STRONG CONVICTION

AN ELIZABETH STRONG MYSTERY

K.C. TURNER

E.M. HANDLY

TWO TEN PRESS

This book is a work of fiction. All of the characters, organizations, and events portrayed in this novel are either products of the author's imagination or are used fictitiously.

STRONG CONVICTION
Elizabeth Strong Mystery Book 3

E.M. Handly
writing as
K.C. Turner

Published by Two Ten Press

eBook ISBN: 978-1-7367415-4-2
Print ISBN: 978-1-7367415-5-9

TRIGGER WARNINGS

The Elizabeth Strong Mystery Series deals with topics that may be sensitive or triggering for some readers, including but not limited to domestic violence, sexual assault, abuse and other criminal activity.

If you or someone you know needs support, please reach out for help. If you have an emergency, do not hesitate to call 911.

National Domestic Violence Hotline
800-799-7233
National Sexual Assault Hotline
800-656-4673
National Hotline for Mental Health and Suicide Prevention
800-273-TALK (8255)

National Human Trafficking Hotline
888-373-7888 or text 233733

CHAPTER 1

*E*lizabeth sat comfortably in the back seat of her father's Cadillac staring out the window as she listened to her parents lovingly bicker back and forth. Visibility was weakened due to the falling snow. No one was happy to return to Ohio earlier than expected, especially with the first winter storm arriving so soon.

Sighing as she placed her head on the headrest, she could hear slight frustration in her mother's voice. "Desmond, all I'm saying is, James could have been more understanding. There is no reason you could not have handled this through a video conference with the client. Four more days and you would have been back in the office. We're on *vacation*, Des."

"Marybeth, I've tried to explain it to you and I've apologized. What more would you like me to do?"

"Frankly? I'd like you to sell your portion and retire. Elizabeth needs us."

Rolling her eyes, Elizabeth chimed in. "Mom, please don't bring me into this."

Her father grunted. "Elizabeth will be fine. She's a Strong."

Perking up in her seat, she reminded her parents, "Hello! I am right here, you know?"

With concern in her voice, Marybeth said, "Des, you might want to slow down dear. Des, slow down, please!"

Moving to the center of the backseat so she could see better, Elizabeth questioned her parents, "What's going on?"

Her father pressed on the brakes repeatedly before he began to panic. "The brakes aren't working!"

There was desperation in her mother's voice as she braced herself. "Desmond? Des-mooond!"

In slow motion, Elizabeth witnessed the vehicle slide sideways into a pile of snow covered, mangled metal in the middle of the highway. Her head violently swinging forward then back again. The gut-wrenching sound of the shattered windshield rang in her ears as shards of glass flew through the car towards her face like glistening chunks of ice, mixed with flakes of snow. With the first slice of her skin, she woke abruptly, her fingernail catching her cheek as she swiftly pushed her sleep mask from her eyes to her forehead. "Mom!" she screamed looking for comfort.

The cold air shook the windows. Elizabeth squinted at the clock on her nightstand. 7:10 am. She'd overslept. "Shit!" With no time to feel sorry for herself, she flung the blankets off her body, leapt out of bed, and ran to the coffee pot. It had already shut itself off. She poured the brewed coffee back into the water well and turned the pot back on before hustling to the bathroom. Pinning her long blonde hair into a clip, she quickly rinsed herself in the shower.

Shivering as she dried herself off, she pulled a white sailor sweater over her head and jumped into a pair of skinny khakis before brushing her hair and placing minimal makeup on her face. Her toes began to cringe at the cold tile floor, making her dash to the bedroom for a pair of warm socks and her ankle boots. Ready in record time, she poured herself a cup of coffee into a to-go mug, threw on her pea coat, grabbed her bag, and headed out the door.

The dead leaves rattled between her feet as she ran to the car. Jumping in on the driver's side, she turned the key to the ignition. The engine struggled, making her pump the gas pedal a couple times. "Come on baby, not today." The reality of the nightmare seeping back into her mind, tears began to well in her eyes. *Please not today, please not today*, she silently begged as she took a deep breath. As the engine started to rev, she nailed the gas pedal again and switched the heater on high with a sigh of relief. After giving the old car a chance to heat up, she headed to downtown Silverton, Ohio. Driving well over the speed limit, she made it to the office with minutes to spare.

She hustled into the building towards the elevator. It was currently on the fifth floor. While she was waiting, she began to smell White Diamonds wafting through the air. Rolling her eyes, an older lady from the tax map office walked up beside her to wait. "Good morning!" she said with enthusiasm. The scent of the perfume began to choke Elizabeth. Afraid of opening her mouth, she smiled and nodded at the woman, wondering if she would be able to hold her breath to the second floor where the lady would exit. It didn't matter, the stench would last until lunchtime.

Reaching the top floor, she exited the elevator taking in a deep breath and rushing to the front lobby of the office. Andrea smiled at her from behind the bulletproof glass and didn't hesitate to buzz her in. Feeling a little less stressed, she slowed her pace a bit. Walking past Peggy Cabot's office, a wave of dread washed over her as she heard Peggy call out, "Elizabeth?" Stopping dead in her tracks, Elizabeth closed her eyes and breathed in deeply. *Shit! This morning just keeps getting better.*

As she opened her eyes, she took a couple steps back into Peggy's doorway. Before she could speak, Peggy cocked her head with her nose in the air and said, "Nice of you to join us."

China sat in one of the chairs in front of Peggy's desk, her legs crossed and nicely manicured hands set neatly atop her knees. She was careful not to catch Elizabeth's eyes for fear of giving a rude look that Peggy might witness.

It suddenly came back to her the email that was sent out the previous afternoon requesting a morning meeting.

"Sorry, had a little car trouble. Just let me set down my things?"

Crossing her hands in front of her, Peggy's face was stiff. "Sure, we'll just wait on you."

Clearing her throat, China chimed in. "You know, I actually think I left a file in my office. I'll be right back."

Peggy huffed as she heard their whispers down the hall.

Elizabeth looked at China and shook her head. "God, can she be any worse?"

Flinging a piece of her bangs out of her eye, China said, "Try sitting in her office in complete silence for five minutes while she checks her watch continuously."

"Ewe. Sorry. I really did have car trouble. After I woke up late."

"Whatever you do, don't tell her that. I think I need to visit the little-girls room, make her wait a few more minutes." She laughed.

Elizabeth giggled. "You're terrible."

Reaching her office door, China looked back and winked at her friend. "Hey, somebody's gotta keep the balance."

Elizabeth set her things on her desk, took off her coat, and gathered her docket before returning to Peggy's office. As she sat down Peggy sarcastically asked, "All set or do you need more time to prepare?" Attempting to peek out the door she further inquired, "Where did Mia go?"

Trying not to show her frustration, Elizabeth shrugged

her shoulders. She laughed to herself at the fact Peggy was still forced to call China by her real name. An agonizing minute later, they could hear China's clogs coming down the hall. She sat down and shook her highlighted brown hair back from her shoulders. "Whew! Sorry, the coffee is flowing this morning!"

Peggy wasn't the least bit amused. Her cold brown eyes slowly moved from China's face down to her desk, focusing on the docket in her hands. "So, as you're both aware, today I'll be taking over all the cases that have been moved from municipal court to common pleas. We have grand jury coming up in a few of them and I need you both to bring me up to speed on these cases."

China immediately spoke up. "I'm sorry, Peggy, but if that's the case, wouldn't our time be better served if you brought us in separately and went over the cases one on one?" While Peggy wasn't looking, she winked at Elizabeth again.

Irritated with China's assertiveness, Peggy tilted her head back, lightly shook her bottle-blonde, 80s-rock-band hair, and stuck her nose in the air while trying to remain in charge of the meeting. "Well, *Mia*, in order to discuss each case, first I need to know exactly who has been working on what."

Elizabeth had grown tired of Peggy singling China out for everything. It was a valid question. She was also sick to death of her overall demeanor and snotty attitude. She couldn't stay silent any longer. "Peggy, correct me if I'm wrong, but aren't you the Director of Victim Services? Shouldn't you know who has what case?"

Peggy looked down and took a breath, smirking sideways. She turned to her printer, made a of copy of her docket and handed one to each of them. "I've highlighted the relevant cases. Pull your files and leave them on my desk." Not making eye contact, she immersed herself in the file in front of her.

Elizabeth remained seated. "I'm really not comfortable with this new system, Peggy. I mean, we should be following these individuals through to the end of their case."

Peggy shot her an unhappy look. "I frankly don't care what you're comfortable with, Elizabeth. I'll run my division how I see fit. I think we're done here."

Thinking only about the concern for her victims, Elizabeth continued, "Can we at least talk about this? I have a specific victim who has grand jury testimony *today*. I've been working with her for some time now and she's expecting me to be in court."

Without looking up from her desk, Peggy said, "That will be all. I'll let you know if I have any questions about the cases."

China and Elizabeth looked at each other in awe. Peggy finally looked at both of them. "Don't you have work to do?" Her eyes returned to her desk.

China's slanted eyes were wide with surprise as her lips silently told Elizabeth 'wow'. They both rose from their seats and quickly retreated down the hall towards their own offices.

Stomping her feet as she walked, Elizabeth looked to China and shook her head stating out loud, "This is bullshit." She took a B-line to her office and began slamming things. China slid into one of the chairs in front of Elizabeth's desk.

"Liz, I appreciate you sticking up for me in there, but don't risk your job for me. I'm a big girl. I don't need you coming to my rescue."

She stopped for a moment, sat down at her desk, and took a breath. "I wasn't trying to come to your rescue, China. You had a valid question with what seemed to be a logical and more efficient way of doing it. I have valid concerns for my victim who is already deathly afraid to come forward. This new system sucks and it reeks of a power trip on Peggy's part."

"Well, I can't disagree with you there but I don't think there's much we can do about it at this point."

Elizabeth's face lit up with confidence. "Wanna bet?" She rose from her chair, grabbing a file from the desk before charging out the door.

Dread washed over China as she said, "Oh shit," and quickly retreated to her office to avoid any kind of fallout.

Marching down the hall and through the main office, Elizabeth was focused, making eye contact with no one. The secretaries followed the brush of air as she passed. Sensing trouble, they looked at each other and quickly went back to their work. Reaching Marilyn's Bennett's office, Elizabeth crossed the threshold as she knocked on the door.

Standing behind her desk, Marilyn was packing her briefcase in preparation for court. Her tired but cheerful face looked at Elizabeth. "What's up kiddo?"

Grabbing onto the door handle and shutting it slightly behind her, she asked for permission. "May I?"

Knowing the tone presented, Marilyn quietly sighed to herself and stopped what she was doing. "Elizabeth, I have a very busy morning."

Unapologetic, she closed the door. "I know, but this is *really* important."

Picking through the files on her desk, she lent her ear. "Make it quick."

Relieved, she didn't hesitate. "Okay, Sara Brewer. Her husband's case is going before grand jury today?"

Stopping the search for her file, she tilted her head in thought. "Sara Brewer."

"Couple months ago, he beat the hell out of her, chained her wrists together before dragging her out to the woods behind their house. Neighbors called for help and deputies showed up just in time before he likely shot her in the head?"

The memory sickened her. Curling the corner of mouth she said, "Yeah. I think one more grey hair popped out on that one."

Elizabeth nodded her head, her grey-blue eyes boring into Marilyn's as they made contact. "Exactly."

Knowing the sensitive nature of the case, Marilyn gave her undivided attention.

Her heart pumping a little faster, Elizabeth hoped she could convey her argument as passionately as she felt it. Taking a quick breath, she released it and her hands began to move in sync with her lips as the words flowed. "I've been working with Sara since the arrest, Marilyn. This woman went through hell. The bruising on her wrists took over a month to disappear." She paused allowing the severity to sink in for a moment. Counting on her fingers one by one, she continued. "She's been at a safe house since the incident, I've given her numerous resources, we've developed a safety plan, I've been to every hearing with her -"

Marilyn propped one arm up by the other and stuck the tip of her pen in between her teeth, squinting intently revealing the crow's feet behind her glasses.

Taking a short breath, Elizabeth drove it home. "Sara trusts me. She's expecting me to be at grand jury for her." Her heart was pounding. Anxious, maybe even a little paranoid, she wondered to herself, *Did I just get too cocky?*

Marilyn briefly paused, withdrew the pen from her mouth and clicked the end of it before matter-of-factly stating, "Peggy wants the case."

Almost regretting her decision, she confirmed her bosses' suspicions. "Look, I'm not trying to step on anyone's toes here. I understand there's been some restructuring and a new chain of command, but this situation is delicate. My victim? Even more so." Again, she quickly inhaled and exhaled, staving off the unease and hoping Marilyn didn't notice.

With hesitation in her voice, she gave the go-ahead. "Alright. Follow it to grand jury. Peggy's not going to be happy, but I think I'm with you on this one."

Sighing with a sense of relief and accomplishment, Elizabeth said, "Thank you, Marilyn. You won't regret it. I promise."

Walking back to her office, she smiled inside trying hard not to let her victory overshadow her purpose. Of course Peggy was going to be upset. *She's going to be down-right pissed!* She giggled and then reminded herself, *Screw Peggy. This isn't about her.*

Gathering her things, she noticed China had already left for court. She glanced at her phone realizing she only had fifteen minutes before Judge Bennett began his strict nine o'clock docket. *Shit!* She turned to walk out and was startled by Peggy's presence. "Cheese and rice!"

Unapologetic, Peggy stood there, batted her eyes and looked down her nose. "I'm still waiting for those files."

Sighing, she picked up a couple files from the corner of her desk and handed them to Peggy, giving her a half smile.

Flipping the file tabs, Peggy paused for a moment. "There should be one more. Sara Brewer?"

A shock wave went through Elizabeth's chest expecting a confrontation of sorts. Taking a breath, she courageously said, "Actually, I'll be taking care of Sara at grand jury."

Peggy pulled her chin into her chest like a turtle retreating into its shell. "*Excuse* me?"

Her heart beating a little faster, Elizabeth looked at her phone once more. "Sorry, I have to get to Muni. I cleared everything with Marilyn, so I would see her if you have any questions. I guess I'll see you at grand jury?" Walking out the door she left Peggy standing there looking confused and disgusted.

Wasting no time, she hustled out of the office and drove a few blocks to municipal court. The parking lot being rather bare, she parked as close to the doors as she could. With her blood still pumping from the thrill of triumph, the cold November air failed to affect her much until a large gust followed her through the heavy double door as she entered the lobby.

Shaking off the chill, Elizabeth noticed a woman digging in the bottom the large bag hanging from her shoulder. Her long red hair slightly covered the woman's face until she looked up right as Elizabeth passed. Their mutual smiles quickly faded as their eyes locked and time stood still for a moment, while feelings of guilt and resentment flowed from one gaze to the other.

Managing to muster a half smile, Elizabeth remained focused and continued on her path to the courtroom. As she looked back, Danielle DuPont quickly went back to searching in her bag as if the encounter didn't faze her. But it fazed both of them. Elizabeth felt sorry for Danielle because her life was nearly ruined by sleeping with the wrong woman's husband. Danielle felt sorry for Elizabeth because her life was changed forever and Danielle could have helped ease the blow of the consequences. They were forever tied to each other in more ways than one.

Releasing a quick breath, Elizabeth's heels clicked faster, echoing off of the marble floor. She entered the courtroom as quietly as she could, trying not to bring any attention to herself. It was all for naught.

"Good morning Miss Strong! Glad you could join us."

Embarrassed by Judge Bennett's tone, she slid into her seat at the table facing his bench. China shot her a warning look before joining her victim in front of the judge. It was quiet for a Monday. With the closing of the amusement park and the onset of winter, only a handful of people sat in wait for their case to be heard. With the holidays right around the corner, the lull wouldn't last for long.

Elizabeth reviewed her docket attempting to forget about her encounter with Danielle. *This town is way too small sometimes.* There were only three domestic violence charges over the weekend, which meant she could leave early enough to meet Sara and prepare for grand jury.

While highlighting relevant parts of her copies of police reports, she heard the door to the courtroom open behind her. Glancing up at Judge Bennett, she noticed him look towards the door and nod his head without straying from his recital of the current charges against the defendant standing in front of his bench. Turning her head, Elizabeth was pleased to see Angel Martinez peeking his head in and motioning for the permission from the judge to speak with her. Then, he signaled her to follow him into the lobby.

Happy to oblige, she first glanced up at the judge to make sure it was okay considering she was already late to court. The judge didn't miss a beat as he continued explaining the defendant's rights and the next steps in the case, barely acknowledging the partial interruption. Elizabeth entered the lobby and Martinez was standing against the wall smiling at her. He wore his typical black SPD polo and a pair of dark jeans. It all blended well with his light brown skin and dark hair closely cropped to his head. The mere sight of him sent her heart into a frenzy.

"Well good morning, handsome."

"How are you, mi belleza blanca?" He smiled wide. His teeth, even and white, contrasted perfectly against his skin tone.

She pulled her blonde hair over one shoulder and tilted her head in agony. "Oh my gosh, you can't imagine how much better I am seeing your smiling face."

His brows drew together with concern.

Slightly batting her lashes and shaking her head, she explained, "I'm alright. It's been an extremely bizarre, nerve-racking morning. I can tell you all about it over dinner. Say five o'clock?"

"Never thought you'd ask." Putting his hand at the small of her back, they began to walk toward the big steel door separating the police station lobby from the hallway outside the courtroom. "You're going to grand jury for the Brewer case, right?"

They stopped just outside the doorway and she drew a breath before answering. "Oh, I'll be there," she said with a roll of her eyes. "That's a whole other story."

He playfully put his hand in the air to stop her. "Wait, don't tell me. Your victim doesn't want to testify now?"

Smirking, she replied, "No, nothing like that. Peggy wanted to take the case from me, so I went over her head and convinced Marilyn into letting me keep it." She shrugged her shoulders.

"Wow. Nice work. Peggy's probably a little bent, huh?"

"I'm assuming! Honestly, I don't care. But it will be interesting to say the least."

"I wouldn't worry too much about it, but then again, she already has a reputation around here. None of the guys are too impressed."

"Like I said, whatever. I should really get back, Bennett's not too happy I was a little late."

"Damn, why didn't you say anything? I wouldn't - "

Stopping him mid-sentence, she placed her hand on his arm and said, "It's fine. I'll see you at Common Pleas, okay?"

Giving her a sexy wink and smile, he disappeared into the police station.

CHAPTER 2

*E*lizabeth sat at her desk and stared at the clock on the wall facing her. 3:59 pm: Tick. Tock. She watched as the second hand slowly made its way around. As soon as it struck the hour, she grabbed her things and snuck out the back door no one was supposed to use. She didn't care. She didn't want to speak to or look at anyone, least of all Peggy. And while the grand jury returned an indictment in the Brewer case, it didn't stop her from being a tad concerned of the backlash she was sure to receive after Peggy had given her the cold shoulder for the rest of the day. Still, all she could think about was getting home and wrapping herself in Angel's arms.

The drive home was the most peace she'd had all day. At least the sun was shining and the temperature had risen above forty. She pulled into the gravel driveway of the lake house and parked in her spot, leaving enough room for Martinez when he arrived. Leaning on the headrest, she breathed a sigh of relief. Now in her safe place, she gathered her thoughts, grabbed her bag, and headed inside.

Upon opening the screen door to the porch, she noticed something was off. There was a glass vase full of dark, wine-colored flowers sitting in the middle of the wicker coffee table. She smiled as she thought, *Wow, he really knows how to turn a bad day around!* Plucking a card from the middle of the bouquet, she opened the tiny envelope, anxious to read the note. It was blank. In her mind, no words were necessary.

She picked up the vase and put the flowers to her nose, breathing in the intoxicating scent. After unlocking the deadbolt and opening the door, she placed the vase on the dining room table before entering her code to deactivate the alarm system and lock the door behind her. Grabbing her phone from her bag, she saw a text from Martinez that read, "See you soon mi belleza!"

Figuring she had just enough time to get out of her work clothes and put her lasagna in the oven, the first order of business was getting into her yoga pants and comfortable sweatshirt. Once she changed, she replaced her fall table arrangement with the flowers and admired them once again.

Unsure where to put the centerpiece, she took it into the kitchen with her and set it on the counter, turned the oven on to 350 degrees, and pulled everything out of the refrigerator needed for dinner. Once the pasta was ready to go, she took her wooden salad bowl from the cabinet before chopping the veggies. Something was missing. *I need background music.*

Retreating to the living room, she flipped through her record collection. Wanting something upbeat but romantically bluesy, she stopped her search at Nina Simone, Sings the Blues from 1967. *Perfect.* She pulled the vinyl from the jacket and placed it on the turntable. Once the needle hit the record, she closed her eyes and moved her head back and forth as Nina's voice rang through the room. "Do I move you..." She sat there for nearly three minutes while the first song played out.

Once it ended and the next song began, she jumped up and began shaking her hips to the guitar vibrations while singing along, "When you like a fel-la, brrmp-brrmp-brrmp-brrmp-brrmp, tryyy to treat him right. Brrmp-brrmp-brrmp-brrmp-brrmp. Giiive him your atten-tion day and night..." She continued to dance and sing as she opened a bottle of Cabernet, pouring herself a healthy glass. As she was cutting up the vegetables for the salad, she heard knocking. Smiling as she put down the knife, she ran to the door and looked out the blind.

Martinez stood there, handsome as ever, still in his work clothes with a black leather jacket covering his polo shirt. Elizabeth unbolted the lock and welcomed him in. He grabbed her around the waist and pulled her close, closing his eyes and burying his nose in her coconut scented hair. His throat hummed. "Mmmm. Como estas, mi amor?" He looked into her blue eyes before kissing her on the forehead. Looking up behind her, he instantly noticed the large burgundy-colored flowers tinged with black highlights. His body stiffened as he pulled back. "Where the hell did those come from," he asked with a suspicious tone.

Elizabeth looked confused. Squinting her brows together, she was unsure how to respond to his question. The ominous feeling in her chest took over the expression on her face. "What do you mean? I thought -" She turned to look at the bouquet and back to Angel. "I thought they were from you?"

"From me? Liz, I would *never* send you black dahlias," he said as he grabbed her by the shoulders and gently moved her to the side. Approaching the flowers with caution, he demanded, "Where's the card?"

Beginning to get a little shaky, Elizabeth replied, "It was blank. Angel, you're starting to freak me out a little." She went to the trashcan and retrieved the card and the envelope.

As she came back into the dining room, Martinez grabbed the vase and took it outside. She followed him to the side of the house and stood in bewilderment as she watched him toss the entire bouquet into the trash bin. "Angel, what the hell are you doing?"

His brows wrinkled and a muscle in his jaw twitched with anger as his eyes scanned the perimeter. With his hand on her waist, he turned her around and said, "Get back inside."

Deciding not to question him further, she did as he asked. As she entered the dining room, she heard him shut the door behind them and bolt the lock. Then he ordered her to arm the security system. With an arrested expression on his face, he looked into her eyes and insisted; "Don't *ever* enter this house again without turning that on first. Got it?"

"Got it." She nervously nodded her head in compliance. She placed her forehead in her hand and rubbed her temple as she walked past him into the kitchen. Grabbing her glass of wine she took a sip, closed her eyes and tilted her head back, gulping it down. As she opened her eyes, Martinez stood next to her in front of the window above the sink with his hands on the strings to the blind, guardedly looking out before pulling it shut.

"Angel, can you please tell me what's going on?"

Changing the tone of his voice to a more calming state, he apologized. "I'm sorry, the last thing I wanna do is scare you."

Setting her glass down on the counter, she held the stem to wane her shaky hand and moved her eyes to meet his. "Little late for that. *What* – is – going – *on*?"

Moving from the window to the back door beside the refrigerator, he checked the chain lock and the bolt making sure they were secure. "Look, dahlias can be a beautiful sentiment to send depending on the message you want to convey. They're native to Mexico but all throughout Latin America, the world, really, each color has a distinct meaning or symbolism." He placed his fingers on the blind pulling them open to peak through.

Rolling her eyes in frustration she sighed. "Okaaaay?"

"You don't send black dahlias to someone you care about, Liz." Unsure how to ease the blow, he just blurted it out, "They're sent as a warning. They symbolize anger and betrayal."

Fear washed the color from her face and her lips parted to release a nervous gasp.

Without hesitation he cupped her chin and forced her to look at him. "Hey, I don't want you to worry about this. You hear me?"

Trusting the confidence in his eyes, she nodded.

"Consider it handled."

THE ALARM CLOCK went off at 6:30 am waking Elizabeth out of a deep sleep. It was entirely too early considering she didn't reach optimal REM until around three in the morning. She reached over and shut off the alarm before Martinez wrapped his arm around her chest pulling her into the spooning position and burying his nose into her hair. Moaning at the thought of getting out of bed, Elizabeth said, "Thank you for staying with me."

Holding her tighter he replied, "Thank you for a nice dinner, even though the evening didn't go quite as we planned."

Wiggling out of his grasp she turned to face him. "Can't we just lay here all day and tune out everything else?"

"In a perfect world," he said kissing her forehead. He

slithered out from under the comforter, Elizabeth admiring his built frame as he pulled his jeans over his boxers. "I'm gonna go home, clean up, and head straight to the bureau, see if I can't hook up with Johnson and pay a visit to our friend Robinson. Holden knows I may be late. Are you going in to the office today?"

Falling back into bed, she sighed. "Unfortunately, yes. But I am calling Dr. Baker to see if she can move my appointment up to first thing this morning. I'm sure China can cover Muni court until I get there."

Leaning on the bed, he hovered over her. "Maybe you should just stay home? Let me take care of a couple things."

Looking into his eyes she cupped his handsome face with her hands. "You're really amazing, do you know that?" Lifting her head up she kissed him hard on the lips, slid out from under him, and jumped out of bed. "I'll go absolutely crazy if I stay here all day and sulk. Unless, of course, you stay with me?" He shook his head shamefully. "Then it's settled. My mind works better when I stay busy."

He walked around the edge of the bed and grabbed his jacket. "I would love to keep you busy but I'm getting a jump on this before things get out of hand."

She followed him to the door to secure the lock and set the security alarm before pouring herself a cup of much needed fuel. Holding onto the door and leaning her head against it, she looked at him with a grateful smile curving her mouth. "Thank you."

He shook his head as if to say *No thanks necessary.* "That's what I'm here for." Strutting to the screen door of the porch he turned back for a moment and said, "I'll call you later."

SITTING in the lobby of the doctor's office, Elizabeth scrolled through her phone as she waited, glancing up periodically at the door with the nameplate that read *Dr. Laura Lee Baker, MD.* Upon hearing the door unlatch, Elizabeth looked up as a meek looking, young girl walked up to the front desk with her head hung low. Dr. Baker followed behind and met the receptionist, giving her some instructions before turning around and acknowledging Elizabeth. She smiled. "Liz, how are you? Come on back, please."

Rising from her chair, she grabbed her things. "Thank you so much for getting me in this morning."

"It's no problem at all. Fortunately for you, I happened to have a cancellation." Her voice was warm and inviting. They sat down across from each other in two chairs next to the bay window overlooking a private garden. Holding her pad and pen, Dr. Baker looked at Elizabeth with genuine concern. "It's not like you to move your appointment up, Liz. What's happened that brings you in early?"

Threading her fingers together on her lap, tears welled in her eyes. She glanced out at the garden that had been taken hostage by the looming winter.

Fighting the urge to cry she sucked in a breath and said, "Well, I guess the better question is, what hasn't happened." She sighed heavily. "You know, I've been doing so well since he got out. I've tried to live as if he was still in prison, like we discussed, and I hardly need my meds. Work has been going good, considering."

Her pen stopped moving on the notepad. "I agree you've been doing exceptionally well the past few months and I am happy I haven't had to write you a prescription in a couple months."

"I still have five pills from the last one. But as of yesterday, my anxiety level has peaked. Now, I have four," she said with a tone of defeat.

"Liz, it's okay for you to take a Valium when necessary. That's what they're there for. Don't beat yourself up about that. So, tell me what happened yesterday."

Elizabeth proceeded to explain the previous day in detail from her run in with Peggy to the moment she received the flowers. "I don't know what I would have done had Angel not been there. I mean, if he called and told me all of that over the phone, I would have lost my shit!"

Dr. Baker set her pad and pen on the windowsill next to her and gently placed her hands on her lap, leaning forward towards Elizabeth. "I can certainly understand why your anxiety is coming back with a vengeance, but let's evaluate, shall we?"

Elizabeth wrung her hands together. "He's only on the

ankle monitor for a little while longer. And then – he's just out there."

"Remember your breathing exercises." Dr. Baker coached her through the breaths as she calmly practiced with her. "In and out. That's it. Good." She allowed her to take a few more breaths before asking, "Do we know for a fact Steve sent these flowers to you?"

Feeling a little embarrassed, she thought for a moment before responding. "Well, not exactly, but – the fact that Angel found it alarming…"

Resting her elbow on the arm of the chair, Dr. Baker grabbed her chin with her thumb and forefinger. "I understand. And Angel is following up in his capacity as a detective, I assume?"

Nodding her head in the affirmative, she said, "He's looking into it. The card was blank and I'm sure he didn't pay with a credit card, so, you know, I deal with these types of things all the time. Victims call regarding a violation of their protection order and either there is little evidence of the violation or many officers think the violation is so trivial, they brush it off."

"But you are not being brushed off?"

She sighed. "No. But what makes me more special than any other woman dealing with similar issues?"

"Well, it's not that your special, per se. You're lucky; as unfair as that may seem. You should try turning your feelings of guilt into gratitude." Picking up her writing utensils she asked, "How are things with you and Angel?"

Elizabeth breathed in through her nose as if a pleasant

scent marched across the top of her lip. "He is so good to me. It's been a long time but I finally feel like I'm deserving of having a good man in my life. Angel brings me out of my shell. He got me eating meat again, for crying out loud!" She laughed.

Dr. Baker smiled. "I'm really glad to hear that. He sounds wonderful."

"He makes me feel safe. Even with all this."

"So, take those feelings of safety and accept that you are stronger now. Let's say for the sake of argument Steve did send the flowers, I am sure Angel will handle the situation. Aren't you?"

Smiling and feeling a wave of confidence, Elizabeth said, "Of course I am." She turned to look out the window. "I ran into Daniel DuPont yesterday."

Looking at her curiously, Dr. Baker repeated, "Daniel DuPont?"

"Also known as Jenny Doyle. She was the woman who failed to come forward in Steve's trial."

"Ah, yes. I remember. That was the woman involved in the ongoing case with the casino owner, Richard Gardner, this past spring, right?"

Nodding her head she replied, "That's her. I never even met the woman until that case and now every time I see her, I can't help but feel – I don't know – a little bitter, maybe?"

Dr. Baker slightly shook her head. "Understandable. But you can certainly see things from her point of view? After witnessing what Steve did to you, I can imagine she was frightened for her own well-being. Of course, you also have no idea how he treated her."

"Well, we both have an *idea*, don't we? But I get it. At least she's cooperating with the Michelle Gardner case. That should be going to trial in a few more months."

"People can grow and change over the years, Liz. I'm sure Danielle is as much a changed woman from six years ago as you are. Now, how about we address the elephant in the room?"

Elizabeth looked down at her hands and began fidgeting with her fingernails as if she didn't hear the question.

Dr. Baker tilted her head in an attempt to make eye contact. "Elizabeth? How are you feeling about your parent's anniversary coming up?"

"The same as I always do. The nightmares are back." She looked back out at the barren garden. "You know the holidays are the hardest for me."

"I do. But I also know your parents would be very proud of you if they were still with us. They would also want you to live your best life, free of all the guilt you keep bottled up."

"That's a little hard to do when Steve keeps popping up in my life. And, I still believe he had something to do with the accident."

"You can't live your life based on speculation, Elizabeth."

"But what if it's true?"

27

"The investigation proved otherwise," Dr. Baker bluntly stated.

"Investigation? That wasn't an investigation. Faulty brakes? My father never skimped on anything, least of all his vehicles. But no one would listen to me. They thought I was just a stupid kid going through a tragic loss."

"There are some things in life we will never have the answers to. We must accept them as they are and do our best to move forward."

The more she tried to ignore her truth, the more it persisted. "I'm not sure I can fully do that until Steve Robinson is out of my life. Completely."

CHAPTER 3

*M*artinez sat at his desk cupping his chin with his thumb and forefinger. Upon hearing Chief John Holden's heavy footsteps in the hallway, He jumped out of his chair and headed in his direction. "Morning, Chief!"

"Christ, Martinez!" A couple drops of coffee spilled over from his cup onto his hand. "Son of a -"

Opening the door for Holden and allowing him to enter, Martinez quickly snagged a tissue from the desk and handed it to him. "Damn, sorry about that."

Holden grunted as he accepted the tissue, wiping off his hand and the bottom of his cup. "What's got you so fired up this morning," he asked as he took a seat behind his desk in the large leather chair. His hooded eyes looked over his black-framed glasses at Martinez while he sipped his coffee.

Leaning forward there was a critical tone to his voice. "I think Robinson is on his way to getting back in the game, if he's not already there. More importantly, he appears to be flexing his muscles at Liz and it causes me some concern."

Pushing the center of his glasses up the bridge of his nose, he gave Martinez his undivided attention. "Okay, what do you got?"

"Well, my CI has been working with me the past few months on some other things involving Robinson. That may take a little time but we'll see how that plays out. I'm sure given enough rope he'll hang himself. What concerns me is his anger for Liz could cloud his thinking. I already have reason to believe he violated the protection order yesterday."

"How so?"

"She received a pretty ominous bouquet of flowers at her house. You familiar with the black dahlia?"

"You mean the Elizabeth Short murder?"

"Well, yes and no. I mean the actual flower."

"I'm not really a flower kind of guy, Martinez," he said mockingly.

"Look, I know this is a stretch, but I'm positive Robinson sent her the flowers as a threat. The type of flower alone coupled with no note in the card. I'm sure it was him. He wants to rattle her."

Holden shook his head. "I'm afraid that's a long stretch. Even if you had a note signed by him, *maybe* just a hint inferring it was from him, can we even label that as a violation?"

Excitement grew in his voice. "Of course we can. No contact means *no* contact."

"You have a point but I think you're reaching."

"Come on, let me at least look into it?"

Contemplating, he took a sip of his coffee. "Check out the flower shop that delivered them. If you don't find anything solid, let this one slide."

Giving him a thankful nod as he rose from the chair he said, "That's all I need."

Turning to his computer to open the news on the Internet, Holden's voice became stern. "One last thing -"

Martinez stopped just before shutting the door. "Yeah?"

Not looking away from the screen, he said, "- don't bother me again first thing in the morning before I have a full cup of coffee."

He grinned. "Sure thing, Chief." After shutting the door, he returned to his desk down the hall. Detective Shawn Johnson was standing at the kitchenette pouring himself a cup of morning elixir. "Yo, what's up, Johnson?"

Shawn took a sip of his coffee and looked at Martinez over the top of his cup. His eyes looked heavy and tired. Raising his cup, he didn't say anything as he sat down at his desk.

"Damn, dude, you look like shit. Burning the candle at both ends or what?"

Reaching in his desk drawer he pulled out some eye drops and squeezed a drop in each eye. "I guess you could say that." He blinked his eyes a few times and wiped the run-off from his cheeks.

Giving him a look of concern, Martinez asked, "You alright? What's going on?"

He scratched his head beneath his short, salt and pepper hair. "Nah, man, I'm good. Just had a late night is all. Event security."

His look turned from concerned to surprised. "Really? How long have you been doing that? I didn't take you for a moonlighting kind of guy."

"Yeah, me neither but early retirement comes at a cost."

"Huh. More power to ya, I guess," he said shaking his head in disagreement. "Hey, how long's it been since you paid a visit to our friend Robinson?"

Grabbing his forehead and giving it a rub, he said, "Shit, I don't know. I'd have to look at the file. Been a little while. Maybe a couple weeks, I suppose. Why what's up?"

"Well, I was hoping to tag along. I need to make my presence known, give him a little reminder."

"You think that's a wise idea? Holden's been a little testy lately."

"Good looking out but let me worry about Holden. Think you can set something up for the end of the week?"

Sighing deeply, Shawn said, "Awe come on, man. Seriously?

Taken aback by his reaction and growing a tad perturbed, Martinez reminded him, "Dude, you told me before he even got out you would let me ride along and keep it under the radar from Holden. It's been almost three months since his release and you haven't shared any information or even *hinted* as to when you're going to meet his PO for a random search. What's up with you?"

Stretching his neck from side to side he caved. "You're killing me, man." He pulled up his calendar for the week and skimmed over it. "What do you have goin' on this afternoon?"

Raising his eyebrow he said, "I'm guessing I'm going with you to Robinson's?"

"Let me get a hold of his PO and we'll head over there around noon. If anything changes, I'll let you know."

Martinez looked at his watch. It was just after nine o'clock and the flower shop would be open. He stood up and grabbed his jacket from the back of his chair. "Fantastic! I gotta run." As he walked out the door he said, "I owe you one!"

"That line is getting *really* old!" Shawn hollered after him.

Without looking back, he swiftly made his way down the stairs and out into the police station lobby. His sedan was parked right outside the door. He drove to the edge of town to Rose's Garden Shop, parking close to the entrance. As he opened the door the floral fragrances overwhelmed his senses. An attractive middle-aged woman was standing behind the front counter at a long table trimming leaves from flower stems and arranging them in a large crystal vase. She looked up at him with a peaceful smile. "Well good morning, sir. Looking for anything particular?"

Approaching the counter, he returned the salutation. "Good morning! Would you happen to be Rose?"

She continued trimming as she spoke. "At your service. What can I help you with?"

"Rose, I'm Detective Angel Martinez with SPD." He pushed his jacket to the side revealing the badge clipped to his belt. "I was hoping you could answer a few questions for me about a recent order you fulfilled."

Glancing up at him she curled her lips in and pushed them together. "Hmm, let me guess, would this order involve a bouquet of black dahlias by any chance?"

His eyebrows lifted with excitement. "Indeed, it would." Squinting his eyes, he asked, "How'd you guess?"

Almost offended by his question, yet amused at the same time she replied, "Detective, I've been in this business a long time. I've come to know just about every flower there is along with its symbolism. It's not everyday someone calls to send out black dahlias. Seemed really strange to me."

Embarrassed, he hung his head. "My apologies. I didn't mean -"

She waved her hand at him signaling him not to worry and set her trimmers on the table. Taking off her gloves, she circled around to the counter by the cash register. "You would not believe how many women want to sprinkle their wedding bouquets with the black dahlia. It's the perfect fall and winter color scheme, but little do they realize the negative connotations and emotion surrounding it. But hey, what do I know?"

"I hear ya. So, the order was placed by phone?"

"I'm afraid so. But I do have the credit card receipt."

"Excellent!"

"I wouldn't get too excited. There's no name on the card. She used a pre-paid."

Perplexed, he repeated her words. "*She* used a pre-paid?"

"That's right. It was a woman. She sounded rather young. Of course, I could be way off. I can't tell anymore these days."

The wheels in his head were churning. "Do you mind if I take a picture of that receipt if you still have it?"

"Not at all." She opened the cash drawer and lifted the till, pulling the receipt from beneath it.

He cocked his head and looked at her curiously as she handed the piece of paper to him.

"It's all yours. Customer copy." Shrugging her shoulders, she grinned. "Like I said, seemed weird to me."

"Rose, you're amazing." He waved the receipt at her. "I can get more than you think from this." His eyes scanned the shop. "Hey, can I ask you something? How soon is too soon to give someone daisies?"

The laugh lines in her face were now showing due to her big smile. She tilted her head in a motherly fashion. "Detective, I don't believe it's ever too soon for anything." She slowly nodded as she looked directly into his deep brown eyes, looking for his understanding. "However, it most certainly *can*, be too late."

Nodding back, he blinked his eyes once as a grateful gesture before turning to head out.

She smiled at him again. "Best of luck to you!"

ON THE DRIVE from Dr. Baker's office to municipal court, Elizabeth felt minimal relief. The holiday season was extremely difficult for her. But, as Dr. Baker recommended, she needed to remind herself of everything she was grateful for. She was missing her parents but she had many people in her life that cared about her; Marta and Bill, China, and Angel. Her heart fluttered at the thought of him. He - was - a - godsend.

Pulling into the parking lot just after 9 am, she was happy to find it rather empty. That meant a relatively slow day, for the most part. The lobby was quiet with the exception of her shoes quickly clicking across the floor. She slowly opened the large wooden door separating the clerk's office from the courtroom. Taking her seat at the table in front of the bench, she tried not to interrupt the conversation between China and the judge.

Turning from the young, attractive girl in front of him he addressed China. "Miss Lee, I understand your victim is not here today. Have you spoke with him?"

"I have your Honor. I called him earlier and he was unable to come to court today due to work. He said it was necessary for him to go to his office since the defendant took his laptop and he's unable to work from home."

"I see. And where does Mr. Tate stand with all of this, do we know?"

"Frankly, he just wants his stuff back. He's willing to drop the charges if she returns his laptop and the phone that she has in her possession."

The young girl turned to China with disgust. "That's *my* phone. I am not giving him my phone!"

Refusing to turn her gaze from Judge Bennett, China continued, "Judge, the police report is clear. She entered his house without permission with the extra key that he asked for at the time of their breakup. I mean, she wasn't even living with him. And that technically isn't her phone. He advised me *her* phone is on *his* plan, which he is currently paying for."

"Is this true Miss Sawyer?"

The girl huffed and crossed her arms. "He bought the phone for me."

Giggling, China said, "Your Honor, Patrick informed me that at the time of the breakup, she relinquished the phone. Then when she broke in -"

Quickly interjecting, the Judge said, "Allegedly."

"When she *allegedly* broke into his apartment, she *allegedly* stole the phone back along with his laptop. It's all in the report."

Growing frustrated with the back and forth, the judge reviewed the report one more time. Taking off his glasses, he set them in front of him. "Okay, this has already taken too much time from my docket. This is what we're going to do; Miss Lee, you're going to get with Mr. Tate and have him provide proof of ownership on the laptop and phone." He turned to the defendant. "Miss Sawyer, we're going to schedule a preliminary hearing. On the day of that hearing, I expect you to be here having the laptop *and* the phone with you. If you do not bring the items to court, we will proceed with the two felony charges of theft. Any questions?"

China nodded her head and took a seat at the table next to Elizabeth. The bailiff directed the girl out of the courtroom. "This way, ma'am."

Flinging her long hair behind her shoulder the girl yelled, "This is utter bullshit!"

Not amused, Judge Bennett warned, "If you don't agree with those arrangements, Miss Sawyer, I would be happy to proceed today with the charges and add three days jail time for contempt." He mocked her with a snide grin before she huffed and followed the bailiff through the door to the clerk's office.

China whispered to Elizabeth, "If you ever needed a reason to be single."

Elizabeth's phone vibrated. It was a text from Martinez. Smiling, she flashed the screen at her and said, "If I ever needed a reason *not* to be."

Slightly rolling her eyes, China sighed. "Touché."

"I need to see if these victims are here and maybe make a couple phone calls. Are you going to be here much longer?"

"I've got a couple more cases coming up but I should be back at the office before eleven. Why, you wanna grab some lunch?"

"Possibly. I'd like to see what Angel is doing first."

Annoyed China stated, "Of course you would." She grabbed her docket and tried to end the conversation.

Picking up on the tone, Elizabeth coyly asked, "Well, Mia Lee, do I sense a hint of jealousy?"

Titling her chin up and lifting a shoulder she replied, "Maybe?"

"Oh my gosh! Seriously?" she asked frowning.

"I don't know. You've just been spending a lot of time with him. I mean, I get it but I miss our girl time." Brushing off her feelings she flipped her bangs out of her eyes.

Before Elizabeth could respond to China's immaturity, Judge Bennett intervened. "Excuse me, ladies, should we clear the courtroom so you can settle your dispute?"

Embarrassed, they glanced at each other before apologizing to him.

"Miss Strong, can you tell me what state created the NFL?" He grinned with excitement awaiting her answer.

Befuddled, trying desperately not to appear irritated, she looked to China for assistance but she refused to look her way. "Uh, I have no idea, your Honor."

"Miss Lee, would you like to take a stab at it?"

Looking as confused as Elizabeth she muttered, "Um, O-*hio*?"

"That is correct! The National Football League was

originally created as the American Professional Football Association in 1920 before officially becoming the NFL a couple years later. Do you happen to know where they're headquartered?"

"If I had to guess I would say Canton, Ohio, but I'm not positive."

Impressed, he said, "Close but no. Elizabeth?"

Looking around the courtroom as if she didn't hear her name, she turned to him and shrugged. "I have no idea, your Honor. Can you tell I'm a fan?"

He smiled at her sarcasm. "It's in Columbus. However," he said looking at China, "the Pro Football Hall of Fame resides in Canton, so that was a good guess." Turning his attention to his clerk sitting next to him, he continued with the docket. "Okay, what do we have next, Karen?"

As soon as he was finished making them feel awkward, they quietly continued with their prior conversation. Elizabeth turned to her friend. "I'm sorry, I didn't realize I was giving you the shaft. What are you doing tonight? There's so much going on right now and I could really use a girl's night; wine, hot tub, and your brutal honesty." She winked.

Jokingly, she responded, "Oh, so now you just use me for the hot tub."

Elizabeth retorted, "No more than you use me for the private beach!"

She was proud. "Daaamn! Girl is quick with the wit today. I've taught you well."

The judge shot them a disapproving glance before

China took her fingers to her lips and pretended to lock them shut as Elizabeth ducked into chambers to complete her phone calls.

Looking back to the task at hand, Judge Bennett continued with his daily docket. "Mr. Smith, you're charged with one misdemeanor count of assault…"

CHAPTER 4

*D*anielle walked up the back stairs of the casino to the office suite, using her keycard to enter. She tossed her purse on the chaise lounge and circled around the big desk. Plopping herself down in the office chair, she kicked off her boots and wrapped her long legs around themselves. There was plenty to do before her evening shift but she couldn't concentrate. She was nervous, vulnerable, and unsure what Richard's reaction would be when he found out the truth.

It was past nine am before Richard walked into the suite. Just finishing from his morning jog, he rested himself on the sofa and stuffed a throw pillow under his head. "Ah, I love Ohio this time of year!" He turned to look at Danielle and slicked his hair back out of his eyes. "Do you have the numbers from the weekend yet?"

"Not yet. I just got here myself."

Sensing the tension in her tone, he asked, "What's wrong with you?"

Her gut felt like a 50-pound weight dropped to the bottom of it and her heart fluttered at his question. Elbows on the desk, she cupped her head in her hands and bluntly stated, "I can't do this anymore."

Lifting up his head, he looked in her direction and quickly sat upright. "Okay, I'll ask you again. "What - is - *wrong*?"

Before she could respond they heard the lock beep. Smalls walked through the door and nodded at Richard. "Morning, Boss." Glancing at Danielle he turned back to Richard. "Am I interrupting?"

Running his fingers through his hair he composed himself. "What is it?"

"Yeah, uh, I was going over the security footage from this weekend and something seemed off. I just wanted to run it by you."

"*Shit*!" He took a deep breath and stood up to follow Smalls to the security room downstairs.

Now Danielle was nauseous. "Richard, I *really* need to talk to you."

Not wanting to deal with a PMS rant of sorts, he raised his hand at her. "Just - I'll be back."

The two men left the suite leaving her alone and distressed. Her concentration level was nil. She attempted to do the deposit from the night before but it continued to come out wrong each time she tried. She grabbed her hair on both sides of her head and pulled it hard. "Ughhhh!"

When Richard returned to the suite, he seemed to have lost his enthusiasm. He stretched out his neck from side to side and walked over to the desk. Grabbing the arm of the chair he turned Danielle toward him. "I'm sorry I brushed you off." She refused to look at him. Pleading with her, he said, "I told you this wasn't going to be easy."

A tear streamed down her cheek and her teal green eyes met his with a vengeance. "That's not what this is about, Richard."

"Then *tell* me."

Wiping away the tears she asked, "What did Tom want?"

Frustrated he stood up. "You're doing it again."

"Doing what?"

"Deflecting." He began to pace. "For the past *three* months every time I try to talk to you, you change the subject. I know things have been hard since Michelle left, but you have no more on your plate than before."

Shaking her head, her eyes tearing up again she said, "That's not true."

"How so, might I ask? I hired a live-in nanny for Cody, whose mother is probably going to prison for a long time, we haven't begun to plan the wedding yet, and your job here has not changed in the least bit. Please do tell me, Danielle, how has *your* life changed so dramatically?"

Not being able to hold it in any longer, she reached into the petty cash safe, pulled out three huge stacks of hundred-dollar bills, and slammed them down on the top of the desk. *"That's* how!"

"What the hell is that?" He picked up a stack and fanned through it with his thumb. "Have you not been making the deposits?"

Unable to look at him, she informed him, "It's our cut."

Even more confused he said, "Our *what?*"

She took a tissue from the box at the edge of the desk and covered her nose and mouth as she started to cry. "I'm so sorry Richard!"

Taking hold of her arms he pulled her out of the chair and shook her, his sandy blonde hair falling into his angry eyes. "What the *hell* are you talking about, Danielle?"

"I didn't think it would get this far; I swear! I thought he would - he said it would only be a couple times and he would leave us alone."

Realization washed over his face. Furious, he shoved her back into the chair and circled around the desk, pacing the floor. "*Christ*, Danielle! Do you have any idea what you've done?" He stopped and stared out the large two-way mirror looking over the entire casino, one hand on his hip and the other holding his hair back from his forehead. Wiping the stress from his face, he ordered her out from behind the desk and took a seat in the chair. Pushing the microphone to the security room he said, "Smalls, we have a problem. Get up here *now.*"

Within seconds Smalls came through the door. He noticed Danielle sitting on the sofa hiding her face in her hands and Richard was sitting behind the desk, his eyes frantically searching between computer screens. "What's up, Boss?"

"Well, my friend, it seems your suspicions have some merit." Placing his elbows on the desk, he raised his hands together to his lips and centered himself. Releasing a deep breath, he sat back in the chair and looked at Danielle. "Why don't we ask *her* why you're here?"

Raising her head she said, "Richard, please don't do this."

His eyebrows crinkled together. "Don't do this? Don't *do - this?*" Slamming the chair against the wall as he rose, he picked up a stack of money and flung it at her. A jolt went through her body as it smacked the top of her foot. Smalls sternly stood there, arms crossed, waiting.

Gripping the cushion beside her knees she screamed, "*Stop it!*" Richard stood, motionless. Closing her eyes, she took a deep breath before glaring at him, her teeth clenched, she said, "I didn't' have a choice."

"You should have come to me!"

Rising from her seat, she became more confident. "Oh, that's ripe." Walking towards him, she never moved her eyes from his. "And what is the first thing you do? Call him," she said pursing her lips and pointing a stern finger at Smalls.

Stiffening himself, Richard replied, "Well, I don't trust anyone *but* him; and obviously for good reason."

Refusing to hide the offense, she snapped back, "Funny you should say that because the only person *I* trust here is myself." Inching towards him, she begged, "I want to trust you, Richard. I want us to trust each other. But right now, I really need you to trust *me* and let me explain. *Please?*"

Unsure if it was her beauty or some other underlying power, he caved in to her pleas and agreed. "Smalls, can you leave us for a moment?"

Removing his arms from his chest he said, "I told you, you couldn't trust her."

Richard wasn't in the mood. *"Tom, not now!"*

Knowing he meant business by using his first name, Smalls turned toward the door, glaring at Danielle as he left.

Richard turned to Danielle standing before him. "So…"

AFTER FINISHING up at municipal court, Elizabeth and China arrived back at the office together. As they walked through the main office, Mildred spun around in her chair. "Psst! Liz!" She waved her hand for Elizabeth to come to her desk while China chatted it up with Constance.

She sat in her chair with perfect posture and glanced in the direction of Marilyn's office before she spoke. She whispered, "I know you have a meeting with Marilyn before lunch and I just wanted to give you a heads up, Peggy is in there!"

Slumping her shoulders, Elizabeth sighed. *"Great.* Thanks for letting me know."

A devilish grin swept her bright red lips and she winked. "Anytime, sweetie."

Once Elizabeth set her things in her office, she plucked

a file from her drawer and went back to Marilyn's office and tapped on the door.

"Yes?"

Opening the door, she peeked her head in.

"Elizabeth, come on in. I was just filling Peggy in on some things. You brought your file?" Marilyn was seated comfortably with her elbows resting on the arms of the chair, clicking a pen in her right hand.

Smiling she replied, "Yes, Ma'am," and took a seat in the open chair next to Peggy.

Peggy chimed in, "Glad you could make it. That makes two days in a row -"

A tad discouraged, Elizabeth cut her off, "I called and informed Belinda that I had an emergency appointment first thing this morning." Her eyes met with Marilyn momentarily, who sat there quietly through the exchange.

Looking directly at Elizabeth, and irritated at her perceived disrespect she said, "I know you did. However, I prefer you contact me directly next time." She looked back to Marilyn for support. She didn't get it.

"Actually, Peggy, Elizabeth followed procedure by calling the office manager. Shall we continue?"

Shaking off the disregard and looking back to her notes, she said, "Of course."

Elizabeth quietly took a breath and exhaled, thankful Marilyn could see, first hand, Peggy's unnecessary flex of authority.

Getting back to the matter at hand, Marilyn stated, "Okay then. Elizabeth, I was just filling Peggy in on some things in preparation for the Gardner trial. As you both know, this one is a first for this office considering Michelle Gardner started out as the victim and ended up being the defendant. While I was under the assumption the defense would bring up some sort of conflict of interest considering Peggy is now helping Richard Gardner, since of course *he* is now the victim in this case, it appears they are taking a different approach altogether. The defense has filed a motion for discovery and in it they are requesting Elizabeth's victim file on Michelle Gardner."

Peggy responded sharply, "They can't do that. That's confidential information."

Confident in her assertion Elizabeth quickly retorted, "Actually it's not. Unfortunately, Ohio is joined by a few other states that have absolutely no confidentiality statutes when it comes to advocates and victims. Also, Criminal Rule 16 specifically says any evidence favorable to the defendant must be produced."

Trying to disguise her annoyance, Peggy shook her hair away from her face and tilted her head. "Well, I'd have to look into that to confirm it."

Slightly grinning Marilyn proudly said, "Impressive Elizabeth. I'm afraid she's right, Peggy. There is no precedent on the issue, but we are dealing with quite an unprecedented case."

Peggy clamped her jaw tight, trying hard not to show her disdain and remain professional.

Elizabeth's confidence grew. "Thank you, Marilyn. I

had a feeling this was going to come up so I did some initial research."

"Nice job. So, for the duration of this case, the two of you will have no access what-so-ever to each other's file and you won't discuss the case at all with each other. We certainly don't need the defense attempting a change of venue, although I'm sure they may try. Peggy, you and I will work together with Mr. Gardner. Elizabeth, you and I will be working together in case the defense calls on you to testify. I need to figure out what information they're going to use in their plan of attack. I'm assuming they're going to argue Mrs. Gardner suffered from battered woman syndrome but we'll cross that bridge when we get to it. Any questions?"

After a slight pause, Marilyn said, "Okay then -"

"Actually, there is something, unrelated, I would like to address if I may?"

Setting her pen on the desk and crossing her fingers in her lap, Marilyn said, "Of course, Peggy. What's on your mind?"

"Well, with all due respect, I just want to express my deep concern about your decision to keep Elizabeth on the Sara Brewer case."

Elizabeth raised her eyebrows in amused contempt.

Marilyn, instead, looked slightly bothered. "Oh? What is your concern, Peggy?"

Her nose shot up a little higher. "For one, I think Elizabeth's dangerously inexperienced. In cases such as Sara Brewer's, the trauma is so significant there should be someone advocating for her who has experience in mental health."

Elizabeth's heart began racing as the reality of confrontation presented itself. Her smile was without humor as she let out a breath in frustration before blurting out, "You know, not to discount your experience or education but you do not have a mental health degree. You're a social worker and I'm not sure how that makes you better equipped than myself?" She took a deep breath thinking, *Okay, easy Elizabeth.* She shut her eyes for a moment. *I really don't want to get into a pissing match with you.*

Peggy's voice didn't hide her irritation. "I have ten years of experience before coming to this office. You've been dealing with victims for how long?"

Her heart pounding a little faster, Elizabeth continued to defend herself. "I have been working with these women, following cases from Municipal Court to Common Pleas, for the past three years without the assistance of a supervisor. I have a BS in psychology *and* I have a JD. I think that qualifies me." She placed her hands in her lap and wrung them together to hide the fact that they were now slightly shaking with anger. *Deep breaths... In and out...*

Continuing to speak as if Elizabeth wasn't in the room, Peggy persisted with her attack. "It seems her personal issues, past and present, are having a direct impact on her work and frankly, I think she's a loose cannon."

Elizabeth gasped and her embarrassment turned to

raw fury. Her hands clasped onto her file as she tried to contain her rapid pulse, fearful of proving Peggy right.

Rolling the stress from her neck, Marilyn interjected, "Ladies, please -" Her eyes fixated on Peggy, "- before things get *too* personal, this isn't a playground to tout who is better at hopscotch. Regardless of anyone's background, if I didn't think you were qualified, you wouldn't be sitting in your chairs. Peggy, I'm sorry you're unhappy with this decision, but it's final. And save the psycho-analysis for your victims, shall we? If neither of you have anything else worthy of my consideration, I have a trial to prepare for." Grabbing her pen, she returned to the file on her desk.

Her voice quivering with insecurity, Elizabeth knew this was her chance to speak up, "I do have - I have something."

Peggy rolled her eyes in agony.

Somewhat hesitant, Marilyn asked, "What is it, Elizabeth?"

As the words formed from her thoughts, they began to strengthen. "I - I've been mulling over an idea. Even more so since the Brewer case. What if - what if our office provided, not just an advocate, but an actual victim rights attorney?"

Peggy instantly tried to brush it off. "That's ridiculous. There's no funds -"

Putting her hand up as if to silence her, Marilyn, said, "Wait a minute. Go on, Elizabeth." Intrigued, she placed her pen between her teeth and waited.

Her voice still a bit shaky, Elizabeth continued, "Well, I - I just think that some people have a hard time putting faith in us advocates. I believe they get frustrated at the fact that the defendant has the right to an attorney who represents their best interests but they don't have the same courtesy. I mean, of course they have you on their side, so to speak, but they also know that you're not technically *their* attorney. But what if - what if they did have that option, at no cost to them? Why should only well-off victims who can hire an attorney have access to that? It may give some victims, especially in extreme cases, more confidence to follow through."

Marilyn released the pen from her teeth and looked curiously into Elizabeth's blue eyes, mulling over the idea.

Taking her chance to respond, Peggy was all but enthusiastic. "Our department barely has the resources to run effectively as it is. How on earth are we going to gather the funds to hire a victim rights attorney? Our salaries are already mostly covered through specific grants and what *that* doesn't cover, fund raising takes care of the rest. It would take months to get a grant written and gather the money to hire someone." Adjusting herself in her chair, she confidently raised her chin and pursed her lips as if she'd muted any further debate.

"I'll do it at my current salary - until we work out the specifics," Elizabeth bravely declared. She was still shaking inside, but hoped she at least appeared certain of herself. "And of course, I'll need some time off to study for the bar."

Shocked, Peggy gave her turtle face again. When she failed to respond, Elizabeth thought, *Well, that shut her the hell up.*

Marilyn clicked her pen. Her thin lips slowly turned into a pleasant smile, showing another side of her. "Well – I'll – be – damned."

CHAPTER 5

*R*ichard stared fiercely at Danielle. "I'm waiting."

Danielle turned away from him and went to the bar. She normally drank wine but this called for something stronger. Her hands shook as she grabbed the bourbon decanter and poured herself a healthy shot into a rocks glass, taking a large gulp before facing him again. Leaning against the bar she took a deep breath. "Steve contacted me as soon as he got out of prison. Actually, he showed up here the very day he was released. He needed my help and said he would make it worth my while."

He stood there in awe. "And you thought, 'What the hell, let me help out the man who helped screw up my life years ago, so much so, I changed my name?'"

Her teal green eyes shot him a look of disgust as she replied, "Don't you understand? When Steve Robinson asks for something, telling him no isn't an option."

"What did he ask for, Danielle and where did the money come from?"

Taking another sip from her glass, she mustered up more courage. "He sent in a man with a large amount of money to exchange for chips. He would then play the tables, win and lose some, and cash in when he was finished. Steve then gave me a cut. I didn't think it was a big deal at the time. I thought we could make a little extra cash on the side and keep Steve off my ass. But one time turned into two and -"

There was no hiding his fury. "*Money laundering*, Danielle? Are – you – kidding – me!" He swiped his arm across the corner of the executive desk. Paperclips, pens, invoices and other papers went flying across the room along with the apparatuses that organized them. She shut her eyes as her body shuddered from the sound. "What the *hell* were you thinking? I can't - I just can't even begin to process this!" He paced back and forth shoving his hands through his perfect hair.

Placing her glass on the bar she ran to his side. "I'm sorry, Richard! I thought I could handle it!"

Growing more frustrated by the minute, Richard yelled, "Really, Danielle, and how the hell did you think that?"

She was instantly offended at his holier-than-thou attitude. "Oh, I don't know, Richard, the same way you thought you could handle your wife who tried to frame you for murder!"

"*That* is not fair!" He faced her, forcefully grabbed her

shoulders and gritted his teeth as he assured her, "I could lose *everything* because of this!"

Her red bangs fluttered against her brows as he shook her. Her vulnerability was peaking as her eyes begged for a chance at forgiveness. "I can fix it, Richard. *Please* let me fix this!"

Letting go of her, he paced back and forth before asking, "Something just isn't sitting well with me, Danielle. Why would Steve Robinson contact *you*? The one guy – this *one* guy who you managed to *'escape'* from years ago. The man you claim is the reason you changed your name. He just decides to contact you, of all people?" He paced some more and scratched his head. "On the very day he gets out of prison?"

Her body froze and a tear streamed down her cheek as she exhaled from her open lips.

Richard walked around the side of the desk and kicked the supplies lying on the ground, some of them pinging off of the two-way mirror. He sat down in the chair solemnly, thoughts racing through his head. "I think you've done quite enough," he said before calling for Smalls to join them again.

Walking back into the suite Tom glanced at the floor, then at his boss. He looked at Danielle, who turned away from him and walked over to the sofa and sat down, covering her face with her hands. Tom crossed his arms on his bulging chest and faced Richard. "Boss, what's goin' on?"

Richard was smug. "What's going on?" He laughed as

he folded his hands together under his chin and tilted his head at Danielle. "Would you like to tell him, Pumpkin, or shall I?" His lips turned into a malicious grin.

Turning away, she began shaking her head back and forth before wiping the tears from her face and attempting to gain some composure. She stood up and walked back up to the bar. Her back to both of them, she picked up her drink and finished it off, immediately pouring herself another.

"I guess I'll tell him. Danielle, here, thought she would take over daily operations for me and now we have ourselves a *serious* problem, isn't that right, love?" He paused for a reaction from her. He shook his head. "No, nothing? So, Tom, the suspicions you had on security footage you called me down for have merit. Someone came in here with a briefcase full of money and exchanged them for my chips. And within a couple hours, changed it all back in. Best part is, that wasn't the first time!"

Tom pulled his chin back to his thick neck and raised an eyebrow, too startled to respond or inquire further.

Continuing with further disgust, Richard said, "That's right my dear-old-friend, the woman I trusted, brought into my business *and* my bed, has allowed a convicted felon into our sacred space."

Knowing he couldn't say 'I told you so' he was forced to hold back a laugh. Annoyance shadowed his boss' face. Clearing his throat and changing his amused expression he said, "Sorry, Boss. So, what do we do now?"

"I don't know Tom, maybe our new *director of operations* has some ideas on how to handle this very sensitive issue." His sarcasm was piercing.

Danielle sat back down on the sofa staring into the bottom of her glass, terrified to respond.

Deciding to break the tension, Tom spoke up. "What about that new guy, the one from SPD? Lucas, George Lucas."

Breaking her silence, she snidely said, "Seriously? The newbie? What if he was planted here? What if Steve has him in his pocket?"

Tom replied with heavy irony, "Oh, you mean like you?"

Her words struck him like venom, "He threatened me you asshole! Steve Robinson follows through with his threats!"

"Sure thing, Princess. He threatened you with stacks of money?"

Their bickering only made Richard angrier than he already was. "That's *enough*!" Centering himself, he continued, "Although hesitant, I actually agree with Danielle on this. We keep this internal for now and as far away from SPD as possible."

"I actually didn't say that. I think we should involve the police. Don't be a fool and think you can handle him like I did, Richard. Please, I'm begging you?"

"I still find it rather peculiar how he came to contact you." He threw her a cross look.

Closing her eyes, she inhaled heavily. She knew it had

to come out. Pursing her lips she answered, "Johnnie Warren."

The two men looked at each other and then back to Danielle. Both were confused and waiting for elaboration.

"A few months ago, Johnnie Warren, the guy we hired and I had to bail out of jail?" She sighed as if they should know immediately who and what she was talking about. "The kid who was arrested for stalking the victim advocate, Elizabeth Strong. Steve asked me to hire him."

Slamming his hands on the desk he declared, "Jesus, Danielle! This just keeps getting better and better. *That's* why the detective thought it was me the whole time. Entering *my* place of business and invading my personal space. Constantly questioning me as if *I* did something criminal and you never said *anything*!" His hands wrapped around his neck as his head shook in disbelief.

Attempting to explain further, she said, "I thought -"

A single fist hit the desk causing her to twitch. "Nobody pays you to think! Just sit there and look pretty from here on out, okay? First, you're going to give me Steve's phone number and then you're going to vow not to answer his calls or speak with him in any manner what-so-ever from this point forward. Understood?"

When she didn't respond Richard became more assertive. "Un-der-stood!" As she nodded yes, he calmy stated, "Good. Smalls, get three of your most trusted, experienced guys together. It's time for a meeting of the minds."

~

WALKING BACK TO HER OFFICE, Elizabeth could hardly contain her excitement. She stopped at China's door ready to tell her everything but she was on a phone call. She glanced up at Elizabeth with the phone resting between her shoulder and her ear and raised her forefinger asking for a second before returning to the file in front of her to write down some notes.

China giggled at the person on the other end of the line. "Alright, then. I look forward to it." Her face was gleaming with joy. "I'll talk to you soon. Mm, by-ee!" She hung up the receiver feeling a warm glow flow through her. Laying her head on the back of chair, she shook her hair and with an expression of pure pleasure on her face, she took a deep breath before slowly letting it out. She turned to Elizabeth with a smile from ear to ear.

Sliding into the chair nestled in the corner of the room, with dazzling determination Elizabeth asked, "Who was *that?*"

Batting her eyes, she replied in a sexy voice, "*That* was Mr. Patrick Tate and *we* are meeting for cocktails this weekend at that new little speakeasy bar they just opened." She fluttered her eyelashes at her.

"Speakeasy? Well, well, well. Doesn't that sound right up your alley. I heard it used to be an old winery and before that it was a *brothel*." Her eyebrows arched seductively.

Throwing back her head, China's laughter rippled through the air. "Oh, now that will make for quite the conversation starter!"

Elizabeth brought her hand up to stifle her giggles.

China's amusement turned to slight confusion. "Soooo, what's got you in such a good mood? Didn't you just meet with Marilyn and Peggy?"

Shushing her quickly, she whispered, "That's why I'm in such a good mood!"

"Oh, really? Do tell!"

"Not here." She glanced at the clock on the wall. "It's time to eat. Grab your coat and let's walk down to The Dinner. I'm in the mood for breakfast!" She jumped up from the chair, went to her office, and grabbed her things meeting China back in the hall before they walked to the front desk to tell Andrea they were heading out for lunch.

As they got into the elevator China asked, "So what happened?"

Still shaking from her exhilaration, she replied, "Oh my God, I still can't believe what I just did. Pulling her stretchy gloves out of her coat pocket, she gently pulled them on.

"God, Liz, your hands are shaking!"

Speaking rapidly, she explained, "Peggy just totally threw me under the bus in front of Marilyn. She actually said I was a 'loose cannon' and basically said my personal life was affecting my work." She pursed her lips and tilted her head offensively.

"Holy shit! Are you serious?"

"Oh yeah," she said nodding her head frantically. The door to the elevator rang and opened for them to exit. She lifted her hand, "It gets so much better!" Her voice echoed through the main floor so she waited until they walked outside before continuing.

China used her back to open the glass doors leading to Columbus Avenue. Not allowing the cool rush of air to stop them, they headed to the next block where The Dinner and Jared's Java House were located. China's astonished face locked on Elizabeth, anxious to hear the rest of the story. "What did you say," she asked as she pulled out a cigarette, offering one to Elizabeth, which she accepted.

Stopping for a moment to put fire to the nicotine, she inhaled and blew out the smoke, relaxing momentarily. "I fought back! I argued that I had more education than her and we had been doing just fine before she came."

Her mouth dropping to the ground, she was amazed. "Shut the front door!" Grabbing Elizabeth's arm, she stopped before they crossed the street and a deep laugh came from her belly. "Oh my God! That. Is. Awesome!"

"Then Marilyn stepped in and kinda ended that." After catching her breath, she continued, "Well, that's not the end of it."

"What more could there possibly be," China asked with a slight giggle in her throat.

As they stood outside the restaurant to finish their

smokes, Elizabeth told her about her idea on taking the bar and becoming the office attorney for victims. "I mean, I just blurted it out. I don't know what I was thinking."

"Wow. That's a brilliant freaking idea, Liz. I can't believe you didn't think of it sooner. Maybe you would be running the department instead of Cankles!"

"I wouldn't go that far. Marilyn loved the idea and told me to draft my proposal. But if Peggy didn't hate me before, she sure does now and is probably going to make my life a living hell."

Flicking her cigarette butt in the street, China grabbed the door handle and reassured her, "Screw Peggy! She's given us nothing but grief since she got here."

Walking over to an available table against the wall, they took off their coats, sat down, and flipped over their coffee cups.

"It's not that I want her to lose her job; less relevant and kicked off her high horse? Maybe."

The waitress came over, introduced herself, and filled their coffee cups. "I'll be right back over to get your order, okay?"

They both thanked her.

"It certainly wouldn't hurt my feelings to see that bitch leave," China said as she stirred some sugar in her cup before taking a sip.

"Let's not get ahead of ourselves. I still have to pass the bar. The earliest I could take it is in December if they grant my late application, which isn't good for you because I'll be MIA after the holiday to study." Her face was apologetic, "Sorry!"

Abruptly stopping her cup from reaching her mouth she sighed and set it on the table. "Seriously? You're going to leave me alone with her! Ugh." After thinking about it for a brief second, she said, "I guess it would be worth it though." Taking a sip, she said, "Go on."

"I wouldn't even get the results until February. Then I have to wait until May to be sworn in, as long as I pass. We're talking at least six months. And contrary to what Peggy said, that is plenty of time to get funds together." She was proud, but she wanted to change the subject. She coyly asked, "So, who is this Patrick Tate guy?"

"Ladies, are we ready to order," the waitress politely interrupted.

"Yes, ma'am. I'll just have the breakfast special, please. Wheat toast." She was desperate to hear about China's newest potential conquest.

"I'll take the Western omelet, wheat toast as well. Thank you." Turning back to the conversation, she said, "My victim from earlier today. I called him to let him know how things went at court and he asked me out for a drink." She arched her brows seductively.

Pushing her hair back from her shoulder she leaned forward asking, "Uh, the guy you haven't even put your eyes on because he wasn't in court? The one who, literally, *just* broke up with his girlfriend? And with the way she acted in court, seemed like your run-of-the-mill psycho?"

Rolling her eyes, she waved her hand in the air. "Whatever. Besides, I looked him up. He's pretty damn sexy - dark hair, muscular from what I can tell, nice lines in his face, and a killer smile."

"Where did you find him, social media?"

"Of course! And he is on a banking website. He's a financial advisor." She winked.

"Okay. Bonus. But still, please be careful? Remember, he's gone and pissed off some crazy girl."

"Pu-lease, I am not worried about some inexperienced, little girl."

"But still." She gave her a concerned look. "Anyway, do you have plans for Thanksgiving? Marta and Bill are having a bunch of people over and I'd really like you to come."

The waitress set their meals in front of them and made sure they didn't need anything else.

"Thank you!" Placing a paper napkin in her lap, Elizabeth reached for the salt and pepper and said, "They put on a huge spread. Maybe bring a bottle of wine?"

"That sounds great! So, I take it Martinez had other lunch plans?"

Shaking her head and sighing Elizabeth responded, "I guess. I text him and he said he would be tied up with an investigation. He didn't really give me any more details." She perked up, "That just gives me more time with you! Actually, I was hoping we could get together this weekend and have a hot tub/wine night? Tonight, I figured I would go home and celebrate with Angel, if he's available, and then I'm not going to be doing much of anything else but studying after the holiday."

"Of course we could! I can't do Friday because that's my date with Patrick." There was excitement in her voice, "I *know*, depending how well things go this weekend, we could plan a double date!"

Trying not to be cynical, Elizabeth replied, "We'll see how it goes."

CHAPTER 6

*M*artinez sat at his desk watching the clock. Shawn hadn't made it back yet and it was almost time to meet up with Robison's parole officer. Picking up his cell phone, he sent him a quick text. "Dude, where are you?" He relaxed in his chair and waited. No response. He was growing irritated. Putting the phone down he checked his email and his calendar. He picked up his phone again and hit the home button. "Damn it!"

Growing impatient, he decided to send one more text with a mere question mark. Finally, Shawn text him back, "Sorry man. Got held up. Meet us at Robinson's in ten. The address on Washington I sent you." Jumping out of his seat, Martinez grabbed his jacket. Holden was towering in the doorway, startling him. "Damn, Chief!"

Grinning he said, "Payback's a bitch, eh? Where ya headed?"

Although he hated lying to him, he replied, "I got

information on the credit card that was used to buy the flowers sent to Liz. I'm headed over to the convenience store where it was purchased." Technically, he was telling the truth. He was just leaving out some information.

"Nice work. Let me know how that turns out. How are you and Johnson coming along on the Marcus Young shooting?"

He drew his lips in. "Unfortunately, it's kind of at a standstill. Marcus hasn't provided any more information since the last time we spoke to him. We have a facial composite of the perp, but honestly, I think he's jerking us around on the description. He probably owed money on a deal and he doesn't want to hurt his business. Might have to file this one away."

Holden grunted in agreement. "How 'bout you try talking to him once more and then we'll chalk it off as an uncooperative victim?"

Glancing at the time he replied, "Sure thing. You want Johnson and I to tag-team it?"

Pushing his glasses up the bridge of his nose he said, "No need for all that. Just one last college try should do it." He turned to walk back to his office.

Throwing on his coat and following the chief into the hallway, Martinez promised, "I'll swing by the residence after the convenience store."

Without turning around, Holden swung his long arm up and waved.

Hastily running out of the department and to his sedan, Martinez drove to Washington Street and turned down Adams. Reaching Robinson's house, he pulled over to the curb and parked behind Johnson's vehicle, the leaves churning under the tires.

Hearing the vehicle pull up behind him, Shawn exited the car and grabbed both ends of his jacket, zipping it up as he shook off the cold breeze. He stuck his hands in his pockets and walked to the trunk of his vehicle, meeting Martinez. "What took you so long, man?"

Shaking his head, he said, "Sorry brother. Holden caught me on my way out. Where's Stoval?" As soon as he asked the question, a county vehicle came around the corner.

"Well speak of the dirty devil." Shawn grinned as Chris Stovall exited his vehicle. The two men locked hands and pumped fists greeting each other.

"What's up Martinez?" Chris said with a nod of his head. "You here to assist or observe?"

Giving him the same handshake greeting, Martinez replied, "Just observing today, man. Keeping my distance but making my presence known."

"Right, right," said Chris as he nodded. "Alright, Johnson, you ready to get this party started?"

Titling his head and gesturing for Chris to take the lead, Shawn followed him through the yard and up the few stairs to the door of the residence. Martinez leaned on the passenger side of his vehicle and crossed his arms on his chest.

Chris rapped on the screen door a few times and took a step back glancing at Shawn. After waiting a couple moments, Shawn gave him the go ahead to try again. This time, he knocked a little harder. Still no response.

Glancing at his watch, Shawn asked, "You did check his work schedule, didn't you?"

"Seriously, dude? Of course, I did. He was scheduled to work last night and off today. His car is in the driveway and his ankle monitor says he's here." Chris pounded on the door, this time shaking the glass. "Robinson, probation department. Answer the door!"

Just as their patience was wearing thin, they heard the deadbolt click and a 20-some-thing, attractive woman emerged from behind the door squinting her eyes. "Can I *help* you?"

Shawn perked up and flashed his badge. "Why, yes you can! Tell Robinson to get his ass up. Time for a home visit."

Irritation washed over her face as she rolled her eyes. Shaking her head, she grumbled, "Wait here." She shut the door behind her to keep the cold air from leaking in.

Chris and Shawn looked at each other with mutual amusement. Looking back at Martinez, who was still patiently leaning against his vehicle, Shawn gave him an affirmative head nod. He turned back to Chris. "So, how long do we give him before we walk in?"

Before he could respond, the door opened. Steve stood there in a light gray sweatshirt and loose pajama pants, his forearm leaning on the doorframe. Rubbing his bloodshot eyes, he glanced from Chris to Shawn. He opened the door to let them in he said, "Seriously, man? You couldn't wait 'till after lunch?" Gaining his focus, he noticed Martinez. He clenched his teeth making his cheeks convulse.

Martinez was unfazed. He caught Steve's gaze and glared at him. Chris and Shawn entered the residence as Steve held the door for them. Never moving his eyes from Martinez, he slowly shut the door behind them. Chris began walking through the residence, scanning every inch of the place and picking through things to make sure there were no signs of illegal substances. The young girl was standing in the doorway of the bedroom. "Steve, baby, what's going on?"

Stern in his response he said, "Go back to bed. This doesn't concern you." She quickly disappeared, slamming the bedroom door. He turned to Shawn, waved his hand towards the front door and asked, "What the hell is he doing here?"

"Don't give me any shit, Robinson."

Chris finished his search of the kitchen and bathroom before reminding Steve, "Dude, is she decent? You know I have to check in there."

Steve sat down in his chair and hollered, "Yo! Kitten! Put some pants on and get your ass out here."

She opened the door. Already dressed, the young girl walked into the living room and plopped down on the couch, folding her legs under herself. Giving Chris and Shawn a look of disapproval, she pulled her long, brown hair around her right shoulder and proceeded to scroll through her phone.

As Chris searched the bedroom, Shawn stood in the living room, keeping an eye on Steve and his girlfriend.

"Hey princess, how 'bout you put that phone down and go make me something to eat."

Giving him an unappreciative glare, she slammed the phone down on the coffee table and went into the kitchen.

"You sure know how to charm the ladies, don't ya, Robinson?" Shawn shook his head and smirked.

Relaxing back into his chair, Steve said, "So you gonna let that asshole tag along with you every time you violate my personal space?"

"I don't think your PO would appreciate you talking about him like that."

His chiseled face showed no signs of amusement. "You know who I'm talking about."

Exiting the bedroom Chris said, "Alright Johnson, we're all good. Robinson, I just need to check your ankle monitor."

Steve lifted his foot and pulled his pant-leg up as he glared at Chris. "We done here?"

As Chris checked the monitor to assure it hadn't been tampered with, he asked, "Who's the girl?"

Scrunching his eyebrows together he said, "I'm sorry, I didn't realize I couldn't have visitors as a condition of my parole?"

"No," he dropped Steve's foot to the floor and stood up, "a condition of your parole is that you cannot be associating with other known felons. I'm going to need to check her driver's license."

Steve stood up to face him. Chris was shorter, but stocky with a wrestler's physique. "Yo, Kat! Man needs to check your license."

Chris backed up a couple steps and crossed his arms against his chest patiently waiting. Kat stomped into the living room, grabbed her bag, and pulled her license out of her wallet, forcefully holding it out for Chris to grab hold of.

"Alright, Miss Katrina Simons, I need to check your purse as well."

"Are you freaking kidding me? This is some bullshit!" She grabbed her bag, dumped its contents onto the table, and trudged back into the kitchen.

Chris looked at Shawn. "Well, she's a feisty one." He scanned the table and turned back to Steve saying, "Alright buddy. We'll see you next time," before heading towards the exit.

"Looking forward to it," Steve replied sarcastically. He followed the officers to the front door, the screen door slamming shut behind them. He stood there for a moment waiting for Martinez to be in view. They glared at each other before an evil smile formed across Steve's lips and he waved to him before disappearing behind the door.

Pushing himself from the side of his vehicle with his foot, he stood erect and nodded at Shawn. "I'll see you back at the bureau." Shawn nodded back affirmatively. "Hey Stovall, everything good?"

"Clean as a whistle. For now, anyway. Just gotta run a check on his little girlfriend," he looked at his notes, "Katrina Simons. Want me to keep you updated, Martinez," he asked as he opened his car door.

"Shoot me a text as soon as you find out, will ya?"

Chris smiled. "Roger that."

Leaving Steve's house, Martinez continued across town to Nicks Liquor and More. He pulled into one of the parking spaces in front of the store and walked in, setting off the automatic doorbell. The lady behind the register silently acknowledged him as she waited for her current customer to count the change needed to pay for his tall-boy. His Carhartt's were ragged and his hair curled around his stocking cap. Pushing the change towards the girl, he grabbed his brown bag and turned to leave, nodding at Martinez as he passed him.

"How you doin' today," the lady behind the counter asked Martinez, not trying to hide her irritation as she counted the coins and placed it in the proper compartment in the cash drawer.

Rubbing his chin, he modestly replied, "Better than some. Is the owner around?"

The register clanged as she closed it. "Who should I say is askin'?"

Pulling his jacket to the side to reveal his badge he answered, "Detective Martinez."

She looked down at his badge and back up at him, the expression on her face unaffected. "Yeah, sure." She walked to the other side and pushed open the glass door leading to the drive-thru. "Hey Nick!"

"Yeah!" a voice echoed from the back.

"There's a cop out here looking for you!"

"What! What does he want?"

"How the hell should I know," she hollered back to him and allowed the door to spring shut. Walking back towards Martinez she took a seat on a stool. "He'll be right with ya," she said before scrolling through her phone.

"I appreciate it."

When she didn't respond, a tall larger man pushed through the door, this time it swung in the opposite direction. He pulled the hoodie from his un-kept hair and wiped his hands with a rag before shoving it into the pocket of his sweatshirt. Martinez walked around to the beer cooler to meet him, reached out his hand, and introduced himself.

Nick shook his hand and asked, "What can I do for ya, Detective?"

"I was hoping you could help me with a recent purchase from your store." He looked above Nick's head to a camera in the corner that appeared to cover the register area. "Do you keep recordings for that?"

Nodding his head, he said, "Sure do."

"About how long do you keep the files?"

"I keep 'em running for a while. Why?"

Pulling the receipt out of his pocket he said, "I was hoping you could give this a look and possibly tell me who bought this prepaid card."

Scrunching his eyebrows together he bluntly asked, "Now why would I wanna do that?"

"Well, Nick, I believe a very bad man used this card to

send something equally bad to a woman who is pretty important to me."

"I see," he said as he walked past Martinez. He turned around and looked at him like he was stupid. "You wanna look at those files or not?"

Excited, he followed the man. "Yes, sir!"

They walked through to the back of the store and Nick unlocked a door with his keys, leading them into a small office. He sat down in the chair, Martinez standing next to him. "You got that receipt so I can pull up the day and time?" He pulled up the date listed on the receipt and fast-forwarded to the time, going back a few frames to catch the person making the purchase. "Well, call me crazy, but that doesn't look like a man to me," he said as he looked at Martinez.

"No, it sure doesn't." He looked intently at woman in the video. "Can you play it again? Stop it right there." Although she wore a baseball cap, she looked a lot like Steve's girlfriend who answered the door that morning. "But I have a feeling *she* bought it for him." He took a picture of the still with his phone.

Nick closed out of the windows and stood from his seat. "Sorry you didn't get what you were looking for."

Martinez shook his hand. "I got enough. Thank you for all your help." As they walked back to the front of the store, Martinez said, "Just one more thing, can you recommend a nice red wine?"

Nick smiled. "You got it."

~

SITTING AT HER DESK, Elizabeth finished the final letter in her stack to be sent out. At least Peggy had managed to leave her be for the rest of the day. Just as the clock struck four, China stood in the doorway, coat on and bag dangling from her hand. "You ready to get outta here?"

Looking up with a smile, she said, "No, you go ahead. I just wanna finish up a couple things."

Voices from the rest of the office employees filing out echoed through the hall. China leaned against the doorframe with a grin of slight amusement. "I think you've already impressed Marilyn today. No need to go overboard."

"Ha, ha, very funny." She playfully grabbed a lock of hair and secured it behind her ear. "Really, I just wanted to touch base with Sara before I go, see how she's doing since grand jury."

"Okay, have it your way." Spinning on her heel, she turned and winked. "Have a good night. I'll see you tomorrow."

She waved goodbye and got back to the task at hand, dialing the number to the domestic violence shelter. The phone only rung twice before she was connected.

"Safe House Center, this is Loren."

"Hey Loren, it's Liz. Would Sara be available to talk? I've been thinking about her since grand jury and just wanted to check in."

"Oh, hey Liz. Actually, everyone is in a group session

right now. I gotta tell ya, she had a rough night after testifying. But she seemed a bit better today. Just taking it one day at a time."

She sighed and shook her head slowly to herself. "I wish there was something more I could do for her."

"You just keep doing what you do. We all do our part. She's making progress. You know as well as anyone it takes time to build up the esteem and confidence again. I'm sure she'll be happy to hear you called. And I just want to let you know how happy I am you fought to stay on her case. That couldn't have been an easy task for you."

Trying to be modest she replied, "Yeah well, it was important." She paused for a moment wondering if she should share the news. "Hey, not to give away too many details but I have something else in the works and getting your support in the future would be a real blessing."

"Really? What do you got cooking?"

"Well, it's not in ink yet, so keep this between you and I, but I've put the bug in Marilyn's ear about an in-office victim rights attorney; specifically for women like Sara. It would be on a case-by-case basis, of course."

Excited, she couldn't respond fast enough. "Wow, of course! I think that is a fantastic idea and you would have my unwavering support!"

Smiling through the phone Elizabeth said, "Thanks, Loren. That means a lot. Please, tell Sara I called and let me know if she needs anything?"

"You got it. We'll talk to you soon, Liz."

Hanging up the phone, she began shutting down her

computer and printer. Gathering her things, her cell phone vibrated against the top of the desk. It was Angel.

His text read, "Just finishing up here. You up for some company? Have wine!"

She quickly responded, "OMG you read my mind! We are celebrating. Just now leaving. Tell you all about it soon!"

After turning everything off, she finished packing up her things and headed to the parking garage. She couldn't wait to get home. All she could think about was Angel wrapping his warmth around her. But as she stepped towards her car, feelings of dread washed over her positive thoughts. *Oh my God, stop it, Liz! Today is a good day.*

Just as she reached her vehicle, the fear became more pronounced. Looking up over the guardrails she saw him. Not even 100 feet away from the door of the county building stood Steve Robinson, leaning against the light post in front of the bar across the street. He was bigger than she remembered. His eyes hadn't changed. They pierced through her like a knife, sending chills up her spine.

Her breathing became shallow while her heart raced. She watched in horror as he brought his cigarette to his lips, taking a long drag before flicking it into the road. She quickly turned away fumbling in her bag for the keys before they flipped out of her purse and onto the ground.

Crossing his arms on his chest, he watched her with a smug grin of victory before walking to the corner of the street. If it was there before, prison definitely made his cocky strut more prominent. Snatching up her keys, her hands shook as she unlocked the door. Once it was open, she turned back to where he was standing. He was gone and the panic inside her rose to unprecedented levels. Slowly walking towards the guardrail, she leaned over, looking down both sides of the street. Nothing.

She rushed to her car, slammed the door, reached over, pounded the lock down, and started the vehicle. The engine barely had time to warm up and she peeled out of the garage, frantically searching to make sure he wasn't sitting in a parked vehicle waiting to follow her. Instinctively, she did what she told many women before and took a different route home.

Hands clutched to the wheel and knee slightly shaking her foot against the gas pedal, she took turn after turn, slowly making her way to the edge of town. Finding a quiet neighborhood, she pulled off the road to catch her breath. Putting the car in park, she placed her hand back on the wheel, biting her bottom lip in shock. Nervously, she tried to swallow back the tears. She rested her forehead on the wheel and lost all control.

Between the uncontrollable crying, the anger and the fear, her rib cage felt like it was crushing her lungs. Not only was he out, he was going to make her pay. Now she was sure he sent the flowers. That meant he knows where she lives. *Shit! Shit! Shit!*

There was a rap on the window, jolting her from the breakdown with a scream. An old man with white hair, wearing a thick flannel shirt, stood there with a concerned look on his face. He motioned her to roll the window down.

Wiping off her face, she cracked it enough so she could hear him.

"Are you okay, young, lady?"

She sniffled as she wiped her nose with her coat sleeve. "I'm okay. I'm sorry -"

"No need to apologize. I didn't mean to pry; I just came out to get my mail and saw you sitting here. Looked like you needed some help."

She looked over and saw she was parked right in front of his mailbox. "I'm so sorry sir. I'll just be on my way."

Rolling up the window she caught his last words as he backed away from her door, "You be safe now!" Putting the vehicle in drive, she waved at him and drove off.

CHAPTER 7

*T*urning down her driveway to the lake house, the gravel popped, mixing with the leaves beneath the tires. Pulling next to Martinez' car, she noticed he wasn't in it. As she exited the vehicle, the sun was beginning to set over the lake, dragging its warmth into the winter night.

Making her way to the stairs, Martinez came out to meet her. His handsome face warmed her but she couldn't muster a smile. "Hola, bella! Where have you been? I think the wine is chilled by now."

Running to him, she fell into his chest and wrapped her arms snug around his neck. Her nose felt like it was packed with gauze but she could faintly smell the leather from his jacket. Safety. He reciprocated by holding her tight and enjoying the scent of her hair before kissing the top of her head.

"Liz, you're shaking." He tried loosening his grip but

she held tighter. "Hey, hey, hey! What's going on," he asked as he gently pushed her away to look into her eyes. Propping her chin up with his finger, he asked again, "Babe, what is it?"

Her bottom lip quivered and a tear rolled down her cheek. As she wiped it away, she took a deep breath. "Can we just go inside, please?"

Running up the stairs to the porch, the screen door slammed behind her. She grabbed the bottle of wine from the wicker coffee table, entered the security code to the alarm, and unlocked the deadbolt to the front door. Not bothering to take off her coat, she marched straight for the kitchen to get the bottle opener. Martinez followed, locking up behind her.

Taking off his jacket, he carefully folded it in half and placed it on the counter. "Liz, what is going on?"

The cork popped from the bottle and she poured a healthy glass, taking a large gulp. She set the glass on the counter and looked out the window. "I saw him today."

Confused, he asked, "Saw who?"

She took off her coat and walked to the dining area, draping it on the back of a chair. Then she went back to the kitchen and grabbed her glass topping it off before taking a giant swig again.

Growing impatient, he placed his hand on her arm. "Liz, who did you see?"

Snapping at him, she said, "Steve!" She walked into the living room, sat on the sofa, and set her glass on the table.

Cupping her face in her hands she took a deep breath, fearing another breakdown.

Standing over her, anger filled his face. "Tell me exactly what happened."

"I left the office and went to my car. He was standing right across the street glaring up at me - like he was waiting for me."

"Ese hijo de puta madre!" Storming into the kitchen he swiped his coat from the counter, quickly turning back to the dining room. "Lo mataré!"

Jumping up from the sofa, Elizabeth ran to him and grabbed his arm, "What are you doing?"

"I'm going to do what I should've done this afternoon and beat that shit-eating grin right off that cabróns face."

Her voice was stern. "No! No, you are not!"

As he looked down at her, her eyes pleaded with him to reconsider. "Maldita sea! I was just at his house today. He's got balls, I'll give him that!" He turned around, jacket still in hand, and grabbed onto the back of the chair. Turning back to her, he said, "Then we go straight to the station and file a report."

She grabbed his jacket from his hand and laid it on the table. Pulling out the chair she ordered him to sit down. She went to the kitchen for the bottle of wine and another glass, setting it in front of them. Retrieving her glass from the living room, she pulled up a chair and sat in silence for a moment while she poured him a glass. "Look, far be it for me to be the voice of reason, but you know that isn't going to do any good."

Easing up a bit, he took a drink. "At least get it on paper, Liz."

Staring into her glass, she twirled the liquid, leaving a full-bodied film around it. Propping her feet up on the chair she confessed, "I was terrified when I saw him. I could barely drive home, especially once it occurred to me, he likely did send the flowers. And that means he knows my address, which makes me - I don't even want to think about it." Wiping the stress from her face she choked back her tears. "But what I would really like to know is, how in the hell is he getting around town still having an ankle monitor?"

Leaning back in his seat, he said, "That's a good question. And someone is going to answer it." Pulling his phone from his pocket, he saw he had a text from Stovall. "He sent the flowers. No mistake about it. Not that I can entirely prove it. He's got a new girlfriend doing his dirty work. According to his PO, she's relatively clean, just a few misdemeanors here and there. I'll have him check Robinson's GPS history tomorrow."

Disgusted, he laid his phone face down on the table. "I already know what the data is going to show. He's getting it off somehow without triggering the alarm. He has to be." Standing up, he took hold of the arms of her chair and leaned over her, kissing her forehead, and trying to relieve her obvious tension. "You should think about getting a dog. A really big, dangerous dog." Flirtatiously he added, "Or a roommate, maybe? You know, temporarily."

Looking up into his sensitive brown eyes, she tilted

her head back and rubbed her neck with her free hand. Grinning, she cupped her wine glass again and asked, "What kind of dog we talking about?"

Pulling back, he sat in the chair. "Damn, shot down!"

Hooking her hair around her ear, she succumbed to reality. "As much as I love dogs, I'm not sure I want that responsibility. As far as a roommate, I would make - I *did* make - a terrible one, trust me. Frankly, I'm surprised you're still here after everything."

He looked at her inquisitively. "Now why would you say something like that, Liz?"

"Look at us! We're supposed to be celebrating today and instead we're contemplating stronger security measures for my house. As if the alarm system Uncle Bill installed isn't enough." She propped her elbow on the arm of the chair, cradling her head in her hand.

"You know what, you're right." As he stood, he grabbed her glass and set it on the table. Taking her hands, he pulled her from her seated position.

Lacking energy to play along, she remained limp. "Really, Martinez?"

Playfully, he didn't let it bother him. "Oh, calling me by my last name. That hurts, Liz. Come on, come with me." He continued to drag her to the living room, around the coffee table, and stopped in front of her vinyl collection. Making himself comfortable on the corner of the sofa, he commanded, "Play something for me. Then tell me our reason for celebration. Forget about the outside world for the rest of the evening."

Crouching down to her knees, her spine buckled and she sighed. Looking up at him, she felt the warmth from his gaze and suddenly, nothing else mattered. Blushing, she smiled back and flipped through the covers with her fingers, resting on *At Last!* the debut album of Etta James, 1960. *Totally fitting*, she thought to herself. She carefully pulled the vinyl from its jacket, placed it on the automatic turntable, and flipped the unit on. Once the bluesy melody began to ring through the room, she felt even more at ease. Rising from her kneeled position, she went to retrieve the wine.

Accepting his glass, Martinez thanked her as she sat next to him on the sofa.

Curling her feet under her bum, she graciously said, "Thank you."

His sharp jaw lines and the small patch of black stubble under his bottom lip made his smile that much sweeter. "That's what I'm here for. So, again, what exactly are we celebrating today?" The tone in his voice was genuine and it was refreshing.

Elizabeth proceeded to tell him everything that happened in Marilyn's office that morning from Peggy's blatant disregard for her professional opinion to the petulant argument that ensued. As she spoke, the stress from her encounter with Steve seemed to wash away and the more excited she grew about her plans.

He gazed at her with pride. Shaking his head, he said, "Wow, Liz, that Peggy is a real piece of work. You did the right thing, holding your own. And it sounds like

Marilyn agrees." He raised his glass to her. "Salud, mi amor!"

Tilting her head shyly, she tinged the rim of her glass to his. "Gracias."

The turntable flipped the record to side two and *I Just Wanna Make Love to You* began to play. Martinez set his glass on the coffee table in front of them and reached over to take Elizabeth's glass from her hand while saying, "I think that's my cue."

Releasing her grip from the glass, she caved to his seduction, giving him full control.

DANIELLE STOOD in front of the bathroom mirror, outlining her full lips before applying a deep red lipstick in preparation of wooing desperate men to gamble more money than they should. The entire reason Richard had her working the night shift. And it paid off. Once they had a few drinks in them, all they needed was a beautiful woman to make them feel 10-foot-tall and bullet-proof. And she didn't feel the least bit guilty about it. Men have used her plenty in years past. In her mind, the chickens had come home to roost.

She fluffed her bangs over her emerald eyes and pulled the rest of her red hair over her covered shoulder, showing off the black sequins on her blouse. A single black strap drew across her other shoulder revealing the tattoo of a string of small swirling shamrocks. Rubbing her lips together, she gave herself one more look, smiling back at herself with confidence. Turning to walk out, she was startled.

"Jesus, Richard!"

Leaning his hip against the desk, his eyes scanned from her red Prada heels, up her tight, black, silky leggings, to her sleek crimson hair. "Robinson will be here soon. You should get downstairs."

She cocked her head and pursed her lips. "That's exactly where I'm heading."

As she walked by him, he grabbed her arm, the colic in the front of his hair creating the perfect wave and falling to his brow as he looked into her eyes. Her heels brought her to his height. Leaning over he touched her ear with his nose. "I'm still very angry with you for not coming to me. But rest assured, Smalls and I will handle this."

Facing him, she grabbed the collar of his freshly starched white shirt, straightening it. Her red-tipped fingers trickled down the buttons before resting her hand on his chest. Wanting desperately to believe him, she knew better. "Good luck with that."

His eyes followed her curvy figure as she exited the suite. Pouring himself a bourbon from the bar, he swirled it around the glass and shot it to the back of his throat, savoring the slight burn as the fumes left his nostrils.

Smalls' voice came through the intercom, "Boss, they've arrived."

He walked behind the desk, sat down, and pressed the intercom button. "Your men are in place?"

Smalls stood outside the back entrance with two other large men as the white BMW parked itself several feet in front of the door. Robinson emerged from the back seat of the vehicle as two bulky black males exited the front. "Yes sir," Smalls replied over his blue-tooth.

Richard reached under the desk and unclipped the harness of his gun hanging from the bottom of the desk, giving it easy access. "Good, please escort Mr. Robinson upstairs."

"You got it, Boss." Smalls opened the door and motioned for Robinson to enter.

Grabbing the lapel of his suit jacket, Steve nodded at the driver of the vehicle, who began to follow him.

Stepping in front of the hefty man, Smalls' stern expression failed to waver. Their eyes met in a standoff but Smalls failed to flinch. "Just him," he calmly demanded.

Failing to back off or turn from Smalls, the driver kept his stance.

The corner of his thin lips curling, Steve intervened and said, "It's a'ight, Big D. His house, his rules."

Big D stepped back and rested against the vehicle, his black clothing casting a huge shadow against the white of the car. Crossing his arms against his large chest, he tilted his head back, looking down his nose at Smalls.

Smalls slowly backed away and took the door, nodding at Jon Young, his second in command. A tall and equally fit, bi-racial man. Nodding back at Smalls as he kept his eyes on Big D, he said, "I got you."

Leading Steve up the stairwell, Smalls remained silent. As Smalls turned down to him to make sure he was following close behind, Steve couldn't help but take his chance. "You know, Smalls, I could use a man like you. Shit, with your history, ex-cop - damn man - that would be an advantage in my business. I could totally make it worth your while."

Reaching the landing, Smalls waved his keycard in front of the door to the suite and pushed it open. As the two men stared each other down, he remained quiet, but his face spoke volumes.

Shaking his head and smacking his lips, Steve said, "Pfft, your loss." Strutting into the suite he took a look around and Smalls shut the door behind them, standing guard in front of it.

Richard stood to greet him. "Mr. Robinson, good of you to come. Please, have a seat," he said motioning to the chair in front of his desk.

Flinging his grey jacket to show the firearm attached to his side, Robinson sat comfortably in the plush chair, continuing to scan the establishment. "Nice crib you got here."

Sitting in his executive leather seat, Richard replied, "I do alright for myself." He propped his elbows on the arms of the chair, leaned back, and crossed his fingers in front of his chest. "Let us get right down to business, shall we?" Not waiting for a response, he continued, "Within recent months, you made a deal with my manager to conduct some type of business at the cost of my establishment's reputation. I asked you here today because I regret to inform you, that was not her decision to make, and I am afraid you are going to need to take your business elsewhere." Grabbing the stacks of money to his side, Richard reached over, placing it in front of Robinson and said, "I don't need, nor do I want your money."

Smugly grinning, Robinson replied, "If by 'her' you mean, Jenny, that's right. And I don't really care whose decision it was to make. It was made, plain and simple." His head shook slightly back and forth. "Once you're in, you're in, my man. There's no buyer's remorse."

The impatience was seething from Richard. "Her name is Danielle -"

Steve's lips buckled at his mistake. "Damn, that's right. My bad." Slowly rising from his seated position, he walked over to the bar. Smalls kept a steady eye on him and took a step forward. Richard slightly put up his hand as a red light.

Grabbing a glass, Robinson reached for the ice and turned to Richard, asking, "You mind?"

In keeping his annoyance to himself, Richard kindly replied, "Please, help yourself. I'm afraid *Danielle* was not at liberty to make those transactions. I'm fully aware the two of you have a history, and frankly, I have no interest in learning any more about it - she's moved on. I am here to tell you, today, it's time for you to move on as well and get as far away from my casino as possible."

Taking a sip from his glass, Steve licked his lips and slowly walked over to the large window looking over the casino. "You see that's where you and I disagree." Scanning the bar and card tables below he spotted Danielle. She nervously looked up to the two-way mirror as if she felt his glare. Pointing at her while he held his drink, he said, "That little piece right there actually did you a solid, my friend." Making his way to the chair he sat down, set his glass on the desk, and pushed the stack of money back to Richard. "This is ten percent but my people would like to increase the load. We come to an agreement today, I can increase your cut to fifteen percent."

Resting his forearms on the desk in front of him, Richard's patience was wearing thin. "That *'little piece'*, Mr. Robinson, is my fiancé, and I will not have you referring to her as anything but. Understood? And I don't think you're quite hearing what I am saying. My fiancé *and* my casino are off limits to you. As a matter of fact, I could have my friend Smalls place a call into SPD right now and have you shipped back to Mansfield, where you obviously belong." His amber eyes began to rage. "Don't mistake my kindness and hospitality for weakness. I have people too. They reach from the Great Lakes to as far as the East Coast. And I assure you, they hold more power than you and yours can possibly imagine."

Arrogantly, Steve brushed a hand through his curly black hair and said, "You go ahead and make that call, Richard. I'll be gone before you can spell 'pig'. And remember, your fiancé invited me in by accepting that first payment. It's kinda like a vampire; once you invite him in, he has full reign. So, you can either accept the terms provided, or he just takes what he wants, when he wants." Grabbing his glass, he swallowed the remaining liquor and slammed the glass down, grunting at the rush of fire in his throat. He stood to leave. "Maybe your boys in blue do make it here in time, send me back to Mansfield, of course, you'll also be sending your little girlfriend up the river. Have fun explaining to them how we got this far."

Knowing he was right, Richard failed to show defeat in his expression. "Smalls, show Mr. Robinson out, please."

Reaching the door, Steve turned around. "I have an associate making another drop soon. You have forty-eight hours. Then the offer drops to five percent."

CHAPTER 8

Getting an early start to Friday morning, Martinez picked up his phone and called the probation department. After ringing a few times, the secretary picked up. "Hey Jen, it's Martinez. Is Stovall around?"

Her voice lit up through the phone, as many females did when he called. "Martinez! How are you? You ready for the weekend?"

Slumping in his chair he rubbed his faded neckline with his free hand and tried to entertain her. "I am. It's been a long week."

"You know, a bunch of us are heading to Jimmy's tonight. You should come."

Surprise ran over his face like a shadow. "Uh, well, I made plans for Liz and I later but I'll see what she wants to do after that."

Her response was tainted with embarrassment. "Oh,

yeah, of course. So, I guess if we don't see you, have a great weekend!"

"Will do. Is Stovall there or should I call his cell?"

"Oh, right! Hold on one sec. Sorry!"

Flattered yet annoyed, he shook his head in awe.

"Yo! What's up brother," asked Chris as he picked up his receiver.

"Hey man, do me a favor and check Robinson's GPS for yesterday?"

"Sure thing, what's going on?"

"Liz said Robinson was waiting for her outside the county building yesterday. If so, I mean - I don't doubt her word for a second - but if you can confirm it, that would mean he violated the protection order and his parole, twice."

"Holy shit. Seriously? We were just at his house!"

"Unfortunately, I'm dead serious. Also, I was gonna pay him another visit today. Was wondering if you would come with? Holden's already on my ass about keeping my distance, I don't need any problems if you know what I mean."

"I hear you, man. Uh, let me get with the tracking company and have them send me a report. Looks like he's expected to go into work this morning. If we head over there now, we could catch him when he leaves. You down for that?"

"Don't have to ask me twice. I'll meet you over there. We'll just wait outside for him."

"Cool. I'll have Jen send over for the report by end of day."

After hanging up the phone, they both got into their respective vehicles and headed to Steve Robinson's residence. Within minutes, Martinez pulled up to the curb, parking one door down. Chris parked on the opposite side of the street soon after. The mist from the cold rain tinted their windshields. They left their vehicles running to avoid fog from forming on the windows, which would easily distort the view. Acknowledging each other with a nod, Martinez put his eyes on Steve's door, waiting for him to exit.

As the minutes passed, they both kept looking at their cell phones, watching the time. Finally, there was movement. Steve exited through the front door, securing the lock with his key. Swiftly, Martinez got out of his vehicle and slammed the car door behind him. Chris followed suit.

Reaching the lawn, Steve saw the two men coming toward him. His eyes rolled behind his lids as irritation washed over his face. "Come on, man. What the hell do you want? I need to get to work."

A foot away, Martinez locked eyes with Steve as Chris stood off to the side. "I think I told you more than once to stay away from Elizabeth Strong?"

Arrogantly calm, Steve grinned and said, "I don't know what you're talking about."

Pushing his jacket to the side, Martinez rested his hand loosely on his weapon and cocked his head. "No? That's funny because I have your little girlfriend on video buying a prepaid credit card that was used to send Elizabeth flowers. Elizabeth also says you were waiting across the street from the county building yesterday when she left work. I think that clearly falls within the 500-foot range of the no-contact order."

Stuffing his hands in the pockets of his coat, Steve puffed out his chest and drew his chin up in a cocky manner. "Prove it."

Keeping one hand on his gun, Martinez reached up and rubbed his chin with his free hand. "I know you're getting that monitor off somehow." Focusing, he peered right into Steve's cold, brick-colored eyes. "You're gonna hang yourself, Robinson. And when you do, I'll be there holding the other end of the rope." Turning away, he started towards his sedan.

Chris, just ahead of him, turned Steve's way and said, "Keep it clean, Robinson."

Not moving from his position in the yard, he glared at them as they walked away. "Hey, Martinez!"

Just before reaching the front of his vehicle, Martinez stopped and shook his head slightly, turning around to face Steve again.

"Carlos said to say hi. I guess you and Lizzy have a lot in common after all." The smirk on his face wore a badge of victory.

His boots gripping the wet leaves beneath them, pure rage propelled Martinez forward. Before Steve could move, Martinez lunged after him, pulling his right arm back as far as he could, and with full force crushed his fist forward into Steve's face, knocking him back.

Running over to them, Chris was mortified. "Jesus, Martinez!"

Gaining his balance, Steve bent over and rested a hand on his knee, grabbing his mouth with the other. Looking up at them he laughed and spit a mouthful of blood into the grass. Still humored, he winked and said, "I see you got some of your father's traits."

Martinez lunged after him again but Chris quickly jumped in, struggling to hold him as best he could. Chris Stovall was young and strong, but he was no match for Martinez. "Dude, it's not worth it!"

Steve spit to the ground again and touched the split on his bottom lip with his fingers before gently rubbing it with his tongue. "Yeah, Martinez, it's not worth it." He laughed again.

Chris placed his hands on Martinez' chest, pushing him back. "Dude, I got this!" Turning back to Steve and pointing his finger at him, anger consumed his face. "Robinson, you are *seriously* on thin ice. You may get that monitor off soon, but I have your ass for the next two years. I find out you're tripping the alarm before it's removed or I catch you anywhere you shouldn't be, especially anywhere *near* Elizabeth Strong, you'll be sent back to Mansfield faster than you can plead not guilty. You feel me?"

Wriggling his jaw with his hand, reality struck him for a strong second. "I feel you."

Chris walked back to his car, talking to himself along the way. Passing Martinez, he pushed him hard on his shoulder. "What the hell, Martinez! You know damn well this has to go in my report!" Disappointingly shaking his head, he got into the driver's side of his vehicle and slammed the door.

Devilishly grinning inside, Steve stood there and watched both of them drive away.

Stopping at the first red light on the way back to the station, Martinez slammed the palm of his hand on the steering wheel. "Son of a bitch!" He knew he had to tell Chief Holden about the incident. At least he could try to explain before he found out from anyone else. He was furious with himself for not maintaining control. Making it back to the station, he sat in his car for a few minutes contemplating how he was going to confront the situation.

Knowing there was no easing into it, he shut off the engine and went inside. Thankfully, the lobby was empty. He raced up the back stairs to the bureau, slowing his pace as he reached the hallway, and taking his time towards Holden's office.

The office door was open and Holden was sitting behind his desk going over documents. Before Martinez could knock, Holden looked up over the top of his glasses. "Come on in."

Nodding, Martinez entered and shut the door behind him. "I need to talk with you about something important."

Setting the papers on the desk he adjusted his glasses and gave him his full attention. "Okay, what's going on?"

Sitting in one of the chairs in front of the large desk, he began with his investigation. "I've got information that Robinson sent those flowers to Liz. It's circumstantial at best, but it's still a violation of the protection order." He paused for a brief moment. "So, Johnson and I paid him a visit with Stovall."

Holden shot him an unhappy look. "Now I *told* you -"

Raising his hand defensively he quickly explained, "I didn't get involved in the home visit. I stayed outside but I made my presence known. I thought he needed to know we weren't playing games with him. I didn't even speak to him, I swear."

Grunting, Holden sat back in his chair, sighed deeply and frowned, understanding he wasn't going to like what came out of Martinez' mouth next. "Go on..."

Leaning forward, he explained the urgency of the situation. "Chief, that son of a bitch was waiting for her yesterday across from the county building. He's intimidating her - he's stalking her - *again!*" His coffee-colored eyes were glowing with a savage fire.

The somber expression on the Chief's face echoed in his voice. "Why do I feel this isn't the end of the story?" He leaned on the desk and rested his lips on his knuckles, looking up over the frames of his glasses.

Rolling his neck to ease the tension, Martinez continued. "Stovall and I just paid him another visit. It didn't go as smoothly as I hoped."

Frustrated, Holden sat back in his chair again, shaking his head. "I knew this was gonna happen. So?"

Martinez took a deep breath. "I may have used excessive force in sending the message."

"May have?" After a brief pause, Holden pulled off his glasses and set them on the desk. Rubbing his eyes violently he said, "God damn it, Martinez! I *warned* you – didn't I warn you about this?"

Feeling horrible upon the admission, he tried to explain. "Chief, I know it's no excuse, but he totally provoked me. He brought my *father* into it! I shouldn't have let him get under my skin but it's been a long time since anyone mentioned Carlos Martinez and that's a name I thought I buried years ago." He put his hand through his coarse black hair on the top of his head before gently rubbing his neckline.

Grabbing his mouth, Holden slowly wiped the corner of his lips down to the scruff of his chin and took a deep breath. "I should've seen this coming. This is my fault. I can't say I condone your behavior but I can understand."

"No, this is *my* fault. No need to tell me your disappointment, Chief. I think I've handled that myself. You know, Stovall will have everything in his report. I just wanted to give you a heads up."

"I appreciate that. You know I'm going to have to put you on desk duty for now and let this all blow over?"

His eyes flickered with desperation. "I was hoping we could avoid that."

Placing his elbows on the desk he folded his fingers

under his chin. "How about we wait and see what happens with Stovall's report and go from there? But if Robinson reports you, my hands are tied."

Pursing his lips and nodding his head affirmatively, he said, "Understood." Rising from his seat he walked over to the door. Before exiting he turned to Holden and said, "Thank you."

Holden grunted and released his breath as he sat back in his chair. "Don't thank me just yet," he warned as he shook his head at Martinez as he left his office.

Sitting down at his desk, Martinez felt his phone vibrate in his pocket. Pulling it out, he saw it was Miles Murphy. He immediately answered. "Miles, what do you got for me?"

"Sup, Martinez? You sound stressed. I got somin' for that. Lemme write you a script, yo?"

A slight smile formed on Martinez' lips. "I know you're losing patients with Robinson back in the game but I don't think ambulance chasing members of SPD is your best marketing tactic."

"Ha, HA! Can't blame a brotha for tryin', right? I got somin' for you, for real tho."

"I'm listening."

"Yo, I talked to one of my dudes did a stretch down south with your boy - seem like he know all kina thangs."

Perking up at his desk, Martinez felt a surge of adrenaline pulsate through him. "Is that right? What 'kina' things we talking about?"

"Kina thangs people don't be talkin' bout on the phone, you feel me?"

Sitting back in his chair, his interest grew. "Give me a time and place and I'll be there."

"Jackson Pier. Ten o'clock."

Twenty minutes into the drive toward Lorain, Elizabeth couldn't take it anymore. "Can you please tell me where we're going?"

Smiling, Martinez said, "I figured after the week we both had it would do us some good to blow off a little steam."

"Well, that doesn't quite answer my question."

"Just sit back and enjoy the ride."

They had been quiet for the majority of the time and she could tell something was bothering him. "Are you going to tell me what happened?"

Feeling her concerned glare, he turned to look at her before focusing his attention back to the road. "I made a mistake and caught a little heat from Holden, is all." He didn't want to keep anything from her, but he didn't want her to worry either. When she refused to turn away from him, he glanced at her again. "It's nothing, really." Realistically, he knew his run in with Robinson could go one of two ways and he hoped it was in his favor.

Slowing down the vehicle, he took the next exit and turned right. About a mile down the empty road, Elizabeth saw the big sign that read A & B Shooting Range, LLC. Her eyes widened with joy and there was excitement in her voice as she asked, "Are you taking me shooting?"

Putting on the brakes and turning into the parking lot he said, "I can't think of a better way to end a shitty week, can you?"

Giving him a coy look, she was quick to reply, "Well, I can think of a few but this certainly makes my top five."

He turned off the engine and faced her. Shrugging his shoulders, he said, "You always tell me how much fun you have at China's, so I thought this would make for a perfect date night."

Throwing off her seatbelt she said, "Well done, Detective!"

Walking in the front door of the small, one story building, she found herself in a tiny storefront of every gun enthusiasts' dream. Upon entering, there were two, large floor displays filled with different types of accessories she couldn't begin to identify. Two walls, behind glass encasements full of handguns, were riddled with hanging rifles. Straight ahead, behind the cash register, boxes of ammunition were tucked neatly within their cubbies, reaching close to the ceiling. Directly to the left, a window revealed the front of the range with several empty stalls.

An older, heavyset man with a beard stood up from behind the counter after fiddling with items in the glass case. He adjusted his cap and looked at Martinez with a crick in his neck. "You lost, son?"

Walking towards him, Martinez quickly replied, "I guess that depends on whether you offer any discounts for boys in blue."

The old man walked around the cash register facing him with a stern look. "Actually, I charge double."

Elizabeth's eyes widened as she turned to Martinez, waiting for his reaction.

"Well, Jack, you-old-son-of-a-bitch!"

The old man's beer belly jiggled with his laughter. The two men grabbed the other's right hand and embraced in a tight manly hug, before patting each other on the back. The man stepped back, his big hands cupping Martinez' shoulders. "You haven't changed a bit," he said shaking his head with a wide smile.

His face lighting up, Martinez drew back from him, placed his hand on the small of Elizabeth's back bringing her forward and said, "Jack Cooper, I want you to meet Elizabeth Strong. Liz, this is Jack. This man taught me everything there is to know about guns."

A sense of relief drew across her face. Offering her hand, she said, "Jack, nice to meet you. I was beginning to wonder there for a minute!"

"Good strong handshake for such a little thing!" He bowed at her. "Jack Cooper, at your service."

She gave him a curtsey in return.

Martinez was careful but couldn't help remark, "I hate to say it Jack, but you look a little different since I last saw you."

Taking off his hat and scratching his head beneath the

thinning silver strands of hair he replied, "Yeah, well, since Maggie left me, I didn't see no reason in keeping up with myself. Gotta enjoy every minute. Life's too short to worry 'bout the little things." He walked back around the counter.

Giving the men a few minutes to catch up, Elizabeth scanned the guns in the case, looking for her weapon of choice.

"Man, has it been that long?" Martinez asked.

"Ten years or so I reckon?"

He shook his head in disbelief. "Wow, I - I didn't realize. Is she still in the area?"

"I'm afraid not. The big man upstairs had other plans for her, I suppose."

Lowering his head in shame, Martinez tried to come back from his stupid comment. "Jack, I am so sorry. I had no idea."

"Nonsense!" He managed to put a smile back on his rounded cheeks. "You couldn't have known. It was a small, quiet service. You know I don't like too much attention. So, enough of that! What's your flavor of the day?" He flashed his hand across the top of the glass. "You still a GLOCK-man?"

Moving his jacket behind his waist, Martinez tapped his holster and nodded his head proudly.

Excited, Jack inched his way down the counter and pulled his keys from his pocket. Leaning over to unlock the case, he winked, grinning behind his thick mustache. "Wait till you see this beauty." He reached under the cabinet, pulled out a shiny new black pistol, and laid it on the counter. Nodding his head, he said, "GLOCK Compact Crossover Pistol, Model G45."

His eyes skimming happily over the gun, Martinez was awestruck. "Wow, Jack, that's a nice piece of equipment."

"You wanna take her for a spin, don't ya?"

Backing up a bit, he thought for a moment and took a deep breath before grabbing his chin. "I know what you're doing."

"Oh, come on now. This one's on me. She's a pistol, all right!"

"Twist my arm," Martinez said as they both laughed. "Hey Liz, you find anything?"

Walking back over to them, she was a little lost on what she should choose. Shrugging her shoulders, she said, "I'm not real sure. I mean, I've shot a couple different guns before but there are so many choices!" Looking up at Jack, she asked, "What do you recommend?"

Excited, he winked and said, "Thought you'd never ask, pretty lady."

She smiled and winked back at him before giving Martinez a flirtatious grin.

"What do you have experience with?" Jack asked.

"Not much, really. 38 special, 22 Ruger - Um, I did shoot a 45 once. You know, that Clint Eastwood gun? I think that one was a bit large for me." She giggled.

Jack and Martinez humorously looked at each other understanding the innuendo between them.

Smacking her lips, she was embarrassed. "Guys! That's not what I meant!"

Laughing, Jack apologized. "I'm sorry, couldn't resist. But seriously, I have the perfect gun for you. Cobra 380 ACP. This bad boy is lightweight with little kickback. Shoots maybe 50 yards, six rounds in the magazine. I sell a lot of these to women looking for basic protection. It's a nice little pocket pistol."

Taking the handgun from him, she released the magazine and pulled the slide back, exposing the empty barrel. "It feels nice." Placing the magazine back in place, she sprung the slide shut and aimed the gun at the wall. "I'll give it a try."

"That's what I'm talking about! Alrighty then." Jack winked at Martinez before turning around to pull a couple boxes of ammunition from the cubbies behind him. "Ya think one box a piece will do ya?"

Nodding in agreement Martinez said, "I think that'll do it."

"Okay, grab ya some headgear, there. Stalls are empty so take your pick."

Liz walked over to the wall where the headgear hung and pulled one from its hook in the wall, wrapping it around her neck.

"Those all have Internet radio so just pick your poison and have at it," said Jack.

Impressed, Martinez said, "Wow, entering the world of technology, are ya, Jack?"

Mashing his lips together, he said, "Gotta stay relevant.

And that asshole few miles over, has all the new fancy shit. Can't let him take too many of my customers. Of course, he gets a lot of crazies too. He can have those. All right, I think you have everything you need. Martinez, you know your way around. I'll just be in my office if ya'll need anything."

"Thanks, Jack." Martinez grabbed his gear and led Elizabeth through the steel door leading to the stalls.

They chose two stalls next to each other and laid out their equipment. Martinez showed her how to hit the lever to pull the target towards her. Once they finished setting up their targets, they began loading the magazines for their guns.

Martinez watched as she fed the bullets into the mag like a pro. "You're a natural, Liz. So, what do you think about a little competition?"

"Sounds like you're wanting to lose?" She grinned as she loaded the last few bullets and clipped the magazine into place.

"Oh, it's on Elizabeth Strong! Start at 20 yards? See who's the better shot. I'll only let off six rounds to match you."

Pulling a scrunchie out of her bag, she wrapped her hair up in a loose bun behind her head. Setting her headgear to Black Sabbath Radio, she placed it on her ears and *Sabbath, Bloody Sabbath* rang through the speakers. She turned up the volume and nodded at Martinez. Flipping the switch on the wall, the target drug twenty yards down the conveyor before coming to a halt. She closed her eyes and felt the rhythm of the music moving her head to the tune. Looking over at Martinez she pulled the slide to the weapon back, chambering the first round.

The bullets rang through the steel walls piercing the paper targets. They continued to shoot until she had to reload. After the last bullet left the barrel, she placed her gun on the metal shelf and pulled her headset around her neck.

Martinez had already finished and stood at the side of the stall beside her, watching with pride. He took off his headgear, shaking his head affirmatively as he said, "Wow! Not bad, not bad at all."

"Damn that felt good!" She flipped the switch again, bringing the target back to her. Three chest shots, one to the head, and two more just pierced the shoulder. "Okay, Detective, let's see yours, shall we?"

Moving over to his stall, he hit the lever on the wall moving his target back to them: Four chest shots, two to the head. Elizabeth stared at the target for a moment. "Well, I would hope you didn't miss. My life might depend on it one day." She winked at him and grinned.

The truth of her statement stung him for a brief moment. "I've been doing this a long time. But I have to admit, for not shooting too often or having much experience, you're a pretty good shot. For a girl." His lips curled with sarcasm.

"That's what they call Girl Power." She lifted brows seductively. "Okay, round one is yours. Let's try it again, shall we? We have an hour, right?"

He winked at her. "So, what do I get if I win?"

"Oh-ho-ho, are we offering prizes of sorts?"

Covering his ears with the headgear, he said, "But of course!" He winked at her at stepped back into his stall.

For nearly an hour they blew through their ammunition and joked with each other back and forth. Before they knew it, it was just about time to pack up. On their last round, Martinez said, "Okay, Liz, how about this, whoever wins this round, buys dinner?"

"Deal!" She loaded her weapon one last time, looked over to him and shook her head, curling the corner of her lips in a challenging manner.

Both of them took their stances and began, the bullets charging through the paper targets. Once the last round was fired, they took off their ear protection and brought the targets back to the helm. Removing them from the clip, they compared.

Martinez was yet again impressed. "I don't know Liz, looks pretty close to me."

Laughing she asked, "What do you mean? Mine is clearly better!"

Hesitant, he said, "I don't know about that! Maybe we should ask Jack to settle this?"

"Angel Martinez, are you going to be a sore loser?"

"Not at all! Just saying."

Carefully gathering all their equipment, they walked back into the shop. Elizabeth shook her ears with her fingers to get some normal sound back. Jack emerged from his office upon hearing their laughter and banter.

"Well, how was it? Blow off some much-needed steam did ya?" His smile was wide enough to see through his thick stash this time.

Martinez placed the GLOCK onto the counter. "Jack, that is one hell of a weapon! Clean shot, for sure." He put the two targets on top of the gun. "But I'm afraid you're going to have to settle our little argument. Who has the best target out of these two?"

Taken aback Jack responded, "Oh now, I'm afraid I can't do that!"

Shocked, Martinez said, "Hey, I've got dinner riding on this! Help a brother out!"

Elizabeth stood there, arms crossed, eyes glaring at Jack.

Jack looked at her and back to Martinez. "Sorry, son. Looks like you've got to take the little lady out tonight."

Excited, Elizabeth clapped her hands together and yelled out, "Hot damn! I knew I liked you, Jack."

Martinez was a tad defeated. "Okay, okay, I see how it is." He laughed.

Jack tilted his head. "Sorry brother, but a win is a win. So, instead of being a sore loser, how bout I wrap up that GLOCK for you?"

"Man, I'll tell you Jack, that is a beautiful piece of machinery. But I'm gonna have to pass this time. However, you can wrap up hers for me. Give me a box of ammo too." He turned to Elizabeth, and winked.

Her mouth dropped a little. Before she could speak, he shook his head warning her not to argue with him.

Taking a breath, she closed her mouth and smiled awkwardly.

Jack finished ringing up the transaction and offered them a coupon for an hour of target practice on their next visit. "It was so good to see you Martinez. Don't be a stranger for so long next time."

After saying their good byes, the two of them left the shop and got into Martinez' sedan. Holding the heavy bag in her hand, she couldn't keep quiet any longer. "What the hell was that, Angel?"

"Well, the way I see it, you didn't sound too keen on the whole dog idea, and you seemed even less interested in having a roommate, so, this is the next best thing."

She was a little embarrassed since he brought it up again. "It's nothing personal, you know."

"Hey, you don't have to explain anything to me. It was a shot in the dark. I know it's soon, but I just thought -"

She looked into his brown eyes and graciously said, "I am very thankful. Of course, shooting guns at China's is one thing, having a gun in my house? Well…"

"I get it. I'm sorry. I should have asked."

"No, no. Don't get me wrong, I should probably have a bit more protection. It just makes me nervous to even think I may have to use it. That's all. Honestly, I don't want to think about it at all. But I also understand the reality I now face. I thought I had at least a couple more years but it is what it is."

He started the engine and felt bad for what he did. "I'm sorry. I didn't mean -"

"Don't apologize for doing something good. I really appreciate it. You just have to help me figure out where to keep this bad boy."

He put the vehicle in reverse and backed out of the parking lot onto the road. "Okay, enough talk about that. Next stop, food."

"A metal killing machine may not be the way to my heart but food certainly is! Are you planning on staying with me tonight?"

"I wish I could but I need to meet my CI later. He has some new information for me and it seemed important. What about tomorrow?"

"That kinda stinks because I promised China we would get together for a girl's night with some wine in her hot tub. And I'm sorry, but I can't possibly pass up a hot tub night."

"I can understand that. I guess that means dinner has to make up for the rest of the weekend and I have the perfect place." He grinned.

PULLING down the gravel driveway to the lake house, Martinez sighed that he had to leave her so soon. "Sorry, I can't stay. But I had an awesome night. You really are a good shot. I wish half of our department could hit a target as well as you."

Blushing, she accepted his compliment. "I appreciate that. Thank you for everything, Angel. Really. It's a nice weapon. You know, a while back I even asked China if I could borrow one of her guns to keep here."

He was somewhat surprised. "Is that right?"

"I did. I just didn't want to admit it."

"Well, no one should have to borrow a weapon. Everyone should have a form of home protection. And now you do." She leaned over and kissed him on his full lips. His eyes rolled under his lids at her touch. "I *really* wish I could stay."

She opened her eyes and looked into his. "Me too. But it seems important."

He stared deeply into her blue eyes. "Everything is important when it comes to you."

Blushing again, she opened the car door to exit.

"Let me walk you in." He exited the vehicle, walked her up to the door and into the screened in porch. The night air was cold and damp, but calm. The moonlight on the water gave enough light for him to see the sparkle in her eyes.

She entered the security code and turned her key in the deadbolt, opening the door. "Thanks for a great night. I think I may light a fire, draw a bath, and a have a nice glass of wine. Sounds divine right about now. You go do what you have to do and just text me later okay?"

As she held the door with her cheek, he turned to look at her as he headed back to his car. "I'll do that and I'll be thinking about you soaking in the bubbles."

Back in his vehicle, he tooted his horn as he pulled out. Driving back into town he twice thought about heading back and sinking into the hot water with her. But there was work to do.

Within ten minutes he was in downtown Silverton and turned left into Jackson Street pier where he hoped Miles was waiting for him. As he drove towards the edge of the pier, he saw Miles' large SUV, jacked up on oversized wheels. He backed into the spot next to him.

The window slowly slid into the side of the vehicle door revealing Miles, leaning back in his seat smoking a blunt. He titled his head and blew a large ring of smoke out of his mouth. "Sup, Martinez?"

Turning the lights to his vehicle off, he nodded at Miles. "What do you got for me? This better be good. You have *no* idea what I gave up for you tonight."

Miles smirked and said, "Oh I got somin' for you a'ight. I told you my boy just got back from servin' his time down south. Well, thangs get 'round in the pen, you feel me? Here you thought you had a mole. But you got a bigger problem than that." Swiping his nose with his finger, he looked out over the lake in front of him.

Getting a little frustrated, Martinez tried to speed up the conversation. "Come on Miles, what's so important you called me out here away from my date?"

Nodding his head, he smiled revealing the gold in his back teeth. "That's wus up!" His face turning serious, he said, "Look, man, my boy was in Cell Block C with Robinson and his crew. Said he ran the whole block. Hell man, he ran all dem brothas, the corrections officers too." Shaking his head, he took a long drag from his blunt.

Rolling his eyes, Martinez was growing impatient. "We all know how prisons are run, Miles. What the hell does that have to do with anything?"

"From what he tell me, your boy was rubbin' elbows with the big dogs, you feel me?"

Leaning his elbow on the armrest, Martinez grabbed his chin and looked at Miles impatiently.

"For real tho, you never had you a mole, Martinez, you got you a guinea pig, man. And dem rodents are far bigger and way harder to get rid of."

Grimacing, Martinez asked, "What the hell do you mean a guinea pig?"

Miles smacked his lips in disgust. "*Bro*! A guinea pig! You *know*, a cop dat's in wit the mob, man. You don't know, Robinson working with the mob?"

Finding it a tad hard to believe, Martinez inquired further. "The mob, Miles? In Silverton, Ohio. Come on?"

"Robinson has the cream of the crop 'round here. Shi-it, Cleveland, Dee-troit, To-lee-do." Miles looked at him dumbfounded. His face crinkled. "My dude, how you think he been top dog 'round here for long as he has? He not only got big man backin', he got one of Silverton's finest right in his pocket!"

Shaking his head in disbelief. "I knew the possibility of a dirty cop but one of them working for the mob? In *my* department? Who the hell is it?"

"I'm afraid the length of my information ends there, brotha. Nobody got a name, man. That's for you to figure out. But word is, whoe'er he be, he been dippin' since before Robinson was sent up. Pulled some strings to get your boy out two years early, too." Flicking the end of his blunt out the window, it flew over the sidewalk and into the lake. He sat up and turned the ignition on, rested his arm on the wheel of his vehicle and said, "Yo, that's all I got. Right now, I gots patients to tend to." Miles flashed his fingers with the peace sign and backed away from the curb of the pier, turned his lights on, and took off into the shadows of the streetlights.

Somewhat disappointed, Martinez sat for a few minutes. He got out of his vehicle and slammed the door shut. Standing on the walkway of the pier, he zipped up his jacket and shoved his hands in his pockets, looking out over the calm water knowing his job just got a little harder and wondering who he could trust.

CHAPTER 9

*A*fter a Friday evening all to herself, Elizabeth couldn't wait to hang out with China. It really had been too long. Although she felt bad about it, the past few months she concentrated on establishing a heavenly relationship of sorts with Martinez.

Pulling up the driveway, she noticed the patio looked different. It was completely enclosed. She found the entry and let herself in. Salt lamps adorned a couple small accent tables and candles were lit meticulously around the hot tub with fall deco surrounding the enclosure. The patio itself looked as if it was bigger than before, now allowing for a table that could seat six people. Looking up, she could see the beautiful night sky through the glass ceiling.

China opened the sliding glass door where the old entry into the kitchen used to be. "Heyyy! You made it! I was getting a little worried you were gonna stand me up." She stood there in a bikini with a red robe slightly covering her extremities.

Standing there in awe, Elizabeth said, "When did you do all this? This is amazing!"

"I know right? The contractor finished it just in time for the holidays. I think I'm going to have a kick-ass Christmas party this year."

Swinging her bag off her shoulder Elizabeth pulled out a bottle of red wine and handed it to China. "Has it really been that long since I've been over?"

Crossing her free arm across her chest while holding the neck of the bottle with her other hand, the corner of her mouth curled and she batted her lashes. "In your defense, the contractor was fast and efficient, in more ways than one." She winked. "Anyway, you're here now. Let's get this party started, shall we? Go suit up. There's a robe for you over there and that door right there is a small changing room. I'll open this bad boy up and then we have some catching up to do!"

Impressed even more, Elizabeth said, "Changing room? Fancy smanchy!"

China winked as she turned and went back to the kitchen to uncork the wine.

Taking a glance around one more time, Elizabeth smiled and opened the door to the changing room. She set her bag on the bench and took off her coat, hanging it on the hook behind the door. Although the new patio was enclosed and heated, the air was still cool when it touched her skin. Changing as quickly as she could, she cloaked her tiny frame in the polyester, white robe and shook the chill from herself.

China strolled back into the enclosure with the bottle and two wine glasses in hand. She placed them on the shelf that extended around the entire hot tub and set her phone on the stereo dock, pulling up Internet radio and shuffling the stations. Florence and the Machine began to play. Pulling off her robe she hung it on the wall and stepped into the whirling waters. Letting out a sigh as she sat down, China exclaimed, "You have no idea how much I needed this!"

Shivering as she unrobed and pinned up her hair, Elizabeth agreed. "Me too. What a crazy week. But it ended perfectly!"

Pouring a full-bodied blend into each of their glasses, China admitted, "Well, I know my Friday ended with a *bang*, pun intended," she released one of her full belly laughs.

Raising her glass, Elizabeth's features became animated. "Funny you should say that because mine did too!" Her gentle laugh rippled through the air like waves in the small pool.

"Yes! That's what I like to hear!" China's laughter was as sharp as her wit. "You first. I will almost guarantee my story is more interesting."

"Of course it is." Humor gently rolled across Elizabeth's lips. "First I'd like to know when all this happened." Her arm swept through the air referring to the remodel. "You never mentioned it!"

"You never asked," China bluntly replied.

"Oh, come on give a girl a break, will you?"

"I just wanted to treat myself. You know how bored I get." She shrugged her shoulders. "It only took a couple months to complete. Matt did a bang-up job." China bit her lip, stifling her grin. "Speaking of, do tell!"

Blushing, Elizabeth said, "Oh my God, it's not what you think. Angel took me shooting last night and then we had dinner." She gathered her lips in a crooked smile.

"Now that's my girl, guns and food. Who could ask for a better date?" Cocking her head back she looked to the glass ceiling above her. "Awe hell, who am I kidding - Okay, sorry. Momentary lapse of judgment there."

Elizabeth looked at her awkwardly.

"I'm kidding, I'm kidding! Actually, I'm not but, anyway."

Splashing the water with her spare hand, Elizabeth played back. "China, I'm serious!" She took a sip of her wine. "He bought me a hand gun."

Cheekily, China said, "Well that doesn't surprise me." Crinkling her nose, she asked, "He didn't go cheap, did he?"

"Oh my God," she said with a giggle. "No, he didn't go cheap! Cheese and rice, can't he get a little credit?"

"I'm kidding, Liz. You should have a gun. Kuddos to your Latin lover." She raised her glass to toast.

"I know, he's awesome. I just don't know how I feel about having a weapon. I mean, what if I have to use it?"

Confusion washed across China's face. "Isn't that the whole point? And besides, didn't you at one time ask me for a gun?"

"Asking and doing are two different things. I guess. Right?"

"Liz, don't make things more complicated than they need to be. Steve's out of prison and, obviously, Martinez thinks you need to be protected when his sweet, macho ass can't be there. What's the harm? It's not like you don't know how to use it."

Their eyes locked and Elizabeth didn't feel the need to continue the conversation because she knew China was right. "Okay, so, your turn."

Exhaling with relief, she said, "Finally!" She perked up and situated herself. "So, Patrick picked me up and we went to the Volstead, the place I told you about?"

"Yeah, the bar that used to be a brothel back in the day?"

"Yes! Awe-some little place. They have an entire menu of eclectic drinks based off of old classics and this whole speak-easy vibe, hence the name. I loved it! And the whole brothel story was perfect for a first date to get a home run!" The laughter surged from her gut.

Straddling the hot tub with her arms, Elizabeth listened, amused and relaxed.

"The place isn't very big. Actually, there's only a few tables and a bar, but you can kinda see down this little hall way and there are stairs, and all I could picture was this whole setting, like back in the old westerns, where the ladies would rile up the men, get 'em loopy, and take them upstairs to their rooms. It was surreal, I tell ya! Any way, we ordered our drinks and chatted away. And about an hour into everything, I was totally gearing him up to come back here; one more of those killer drinks and I'm thinking 'this guy is mine' right? And then -" pausing she took a swig of her drink. "And then -"

Growing impatient, Elizabeth said, "Oh for God's sake, China, get on with it!"

She took a breath and prepared herself. "And then – Steve Robinson walked in."

Elizabeth's lips were stiff but she managed to reply, "Oh."

Raising her eyebrows in disturbed amusement, China agreed. "Yeah, my sentiments exactly. The very *last* person I thought I would see or wanted to see on my date. Totally ruined the whole mood."

"Okay, so I'm confused as to why you are telling me this."

"The whole thing was really strange. He came in, sat at the bar, and was flirting with the cute little bartender. And at first, I thought it was just that. But then, when Patrick and I went to order another drink, the bartender told us there was a private reservation and we had to leave. At the time, no one else was there, except Steve. Tell me that's not weird?"

Slightly shaking her head, Elizabeth wasn't sure what she thought. "I don't know, I guess? What the hell do I care what he does as long as he stays far away from me? I guess I won't be visiting this awesome new bar with Angel!"

She let out a frustrated sigh, "You're missing the point, Liz."

Upset that she even brought up his name. "I don't get it, China. I mean, short of you calling the police and telling them that he was in the middle of violating his parole, as if that was an option, what's the point?"

"Well first of all, he totally screwed up my mental focus of getting down and dirty with Patrick, and second, it was just odd how it all went down. Not sure they do 'private reservations' and the little bartender seemed like she was taking cues from him. I have half a notion to call the owner and make a complaint. Actually, I almost called SPD and reported him."

"Pfft, I doubt that would do any good anyway. Even if they would decide to come out for a call like that, he would have been gone in minutes. Hell, I can't even get him on violating his protection order even though he sent me flowers and showed up outside the office! It's utter bullshit."

"I thought your hero was working on that? Is he losing some of his super powers or what?"

Her lips puckered with annoyance. "Yeah, well – this entire week he's been working on it but he's been quiet."

She turned away as her head shook gently. "I just feel like there's something he's not telling me. You ever get that feeling?"

China's eyes widened with caution as she rested her elbow on the side of the tub, holding her glass in the air. "Oh no, don't say that, Liz. The minute you think a man is keeping something from you, you can almost bet he is."

"Thanks, that's just the encouragement I needed." Gulping back the last of her drink she put out her glass and motioned China to replenish it.

Fulfilling the silent request, she said, "I'm sorry. I shouldn't put any ideas in your head. That's just been my experience. I'm just saying, something doesn't seem right with any of this."

"Unfortunately, right or wrong, it seems I'm going to have to deal with the fact that Steve's out and just floating around Silverton doing whatever he wants and there's not much I, or apparently anyone else, can do about it. The only thing left for me to do is be prepared. For anything."

Saturday evenings were the most profitable for Chip's. Danielle prided herself in the clientele she helped to establish since becoming manager. It was the end of her shift and she was doing her walkthrough before going to the office and leaving for the night. Lucas caught her at the cash out. It was nearly three in the morning and the crowd was beginning to disperse.

Flinging her hair over her shoulder, she saw him and said, "Hey Lucas, how's things going tonight? Everything keeping an even keel?"

He smiled at her. He looked much younger than he actually was and he was handsome, permeating a schoolboy type charm. "Yes ma'am. Getting ready to head home?"

"I am. It's been a good night but exhausting. Are you here much longer?"

"Still three hours left on my shift. I believe that's when Smalls is coming back. Said he had to take Richard to the airport to catch the red-eye." His face lit up. "I think I'm starting to be his right-hand man. Left me in charge while he's gone." A large smile swept his face.

She was a little surprised considering Lucas hadn't been there long and Smalls was very particular about his team. And she was leery of him. Lucas was cute but that didn't make her any less hesitant to keep her distance. "I see. Well, that's quite a feat. But good for you, I guess. I almost forgot Richard had to go to Atlanta." She sighed.

"Let me know when you're heading out and I can walk you to your car."

"Thanks, but that won't be necessary. Everything goes in the safe until Monday."

Tilting his head with a confused look on his face. "But Smalls told me -"

Her snotty demeanor took over. "Is Smalls here?"

Immediately, he understood. "No, ma'am."

Giving him a cautious smile, she replied, "Okay then."

Finishing up her rounds, she headed to the office, and made a large drop in the safe. After grabbing her things, she headed down the back stairs to the rear parking lot. Her heels clicked on the cold pavement when she thought she felt a presence. Not quite to her car and fumbling for her keys, she turned to see Steve walk towards her from between two vehicles, her heart jolting through her chest.

His face was stern and he grinned seductively. Moving towards her, his voice became mesmerizingly wicked. "Hey Danielle. Had a feeling we'd meet up like this."

She slowly started towards the car door to escape an encounter. She wasn't fast enough.

He made his way in front of her, pinning her against her vehicle. "Where was your boyfriend tonight?"

The anxiety was rushing through her. "Richard is taking care of some business. You know, I can have security out here is two seconds."

"Ah, yes, security. Where are those fools at now? I'm surprised they don't walk your sweet little ass out every night. Can get kinda dangerous. After all, it is the witching hour."

Gritting her teeth, she asked, "What do you want, Steve?"

"Your boyfriend had 48 hours to make a decision. That 48 hours is up and my offer to him just got cut significantly."

She confidently pushed her face up towards him and said, "He is not going to bow down to you. You're not relevant here, Steve. You stopped being relevant six years ago." Shaking her head disgusted, she raised the corner of her top lip. "Not that you ever were."

Creeping closer to her, he raised his chin. "So, you think because you're getting married to Richard Gardner and have all this at your disposal, you've turned from some peasant girl into a modern-day Cinderella?" He sighed and looked into her eyes with pity. "Oh, Jenny, you'll never be anything more than that sad little girl I picked up at a dive bar in Detroit."

Grimacing from the quickness of her own wit, she said, "That girl hasn't been around in a long time. It appears you haven't changed much, though. Still trying to bully your way to the top of that shit pile."

"You're getting brave in your old age, Jenny."

Cocking her head, she peered into his cold eyes. "From the looks of those marks on your face, seems like I'm not the only one who is tired of your sad routine."

He rubbed his chin before reaching over and touching her cheek slightly. His finger slowly ran down the side of her jaw line. "We used to have some good times, Jenny. If Richard was out of the way, we could run this whole town together." He shot her a twisted smile.

Jerking away from him, her expression was taut and derisive. "You're disgusting. I can't believe I ever fell for you." Watching the frown settle on his face, she took a breath and laughed half-heartedly. "Hell, I can't believe Elizabeth Strong ever fell for you."

A warning cloud settled over his features. Taking a step back, a half-smile crossed his lips as he raised his arm and swung with full force, his hand colliding with her confidence.

Wincing in shock, she grabbed the side of her eye where the back of his hand connected. Unable to breath or speak, she slowly raised her head and brushed the hair out of her face. The fear she felt years ago had revived.

He gazed through her. Savoring the horror that shadowed her eyes he said, "How's that for relevant? I *will* be making my drops. Too bad you said anything about our little arrangement. We had us a nice little thing going. If I need to, I'll bring in more people than I already have. Tell Richard I'll be in touch." He leaned over her as she cowered and whispered in her ear, "This was just my warning shot." Standing up straight, his face taut with poise he promised, "I'll see you soon, Jenny."

She watched him strut away and heavily released her breath. She hustled for her keys and rushed inside her vehicle, struggling to start it. Grabbing the steering wheel, she wanted to scream but the only release she had was silently crying. Pulling the rearview mirror down to see a nasty red mark on the left side of her face, she feared wiping her tears against the tender skin. Gently, she patted under her eye with her fingertips before abruptly stopping to stare back into her reflection wondering how she got here.

Upon starting her vehicle, she tore out of the parking lot and drove as fast as she could out of the city, continually looking in her rear-view mirror fearing he may follow her home. *I'm sure he already knows where we live*, she thought to herself. Hitting the call button on her steering wheel, she asked it to call Richard as soon as the tone sounded that it was ready for her command. Immediately she hung up. He was already angry with her and he wouldn't listen. She knew she had to do something to end this nightmare she created.

CHAPTER 10

*M*artinez walked into the bureau Monday morning with a heavy heart. It was almost as if he knew it wasn't going to be a good day. He turned on his computer and picked up the receiver from his phone to check his messages, when he heard footsteps coming from the chief's office. He shut his eyes and pretended to be somewhere else for a moment.

Clearing his throat, Holden stood in the doorway. "Martinez?"

Opening his eyes, he turned around and managed a grin of sorts. "Good morning, Chief."

Grabbing the back of his neck he swirled it around to relieve the stress. "Not so good for you, I'm afraid. You wanna come on back to my office?" Then he disappeared down the hall.

Knowing it was more of a command than a question, Martinez followed with his head down.

Sitting in his chair, Holden ordered, "Shut the door behind you." After Martinez sat down on the edge of his seat, Holden put his arms out in front of him on the desk and crossed his fingers. His eyes were clear and observant as he looked up at Martinez from under his black-framed glasses and said, "I reviewed Stovall's report over the weekend. Now, I know you don't wanna hear this any more than I wanna tell you -"

"Chief, please?" the expression in his mahogany eyes begged with his voice.

Gathering his mouth in a frown, Holden bluntly stated, "I'm sorry Martinez, I'm gonna need your badge – and your weapon."

Hanging his head in his hands in defeat, Martinez rubbed his temples with his thumbs before lifting his chin and resting it on his crossed fingers. Shaking his head in affirmation of his words, he said, "So, Robinson reported me?"

"No, Robinson didn't report you, Martinez." Aggravated with the response, he slammed his hands on the desk. "Are you dense, son?"

Stiffening in his seat, he came to attention as the look on his face turned blank and he stared straight ahead.

Holden grabbed his mouth and slightly turned his head from side to side. "For God's sake, Martinez, at ease."

Relaxing his stance, his eyebrow curled and his top lip puckered out slightly in anger.

Holden sighed deeply before sitting back in his chair. "Look, it's like this – I'm retiring in the next few years and this just doesn't look good. There are other cases that need your attention right now. Now, I'm fond of Elizabeth Strong too, not as fond as you are of course, but unfortunately this isn't even a case. You have no proof he violated the protection order and -"

"Chief, all due respect, but I *have* proof. I have video of his little girlfriend buying the card to order the flowers. Robinson's pulling the same shit he used to do with Liz; get her to do his dirty work for him. I mean, this guy is calculating, I'll give him that."

"The operative word here is girlfriend. Maybe she's a jealous female marking her territory? You can't tie Robinson to this and you went to the man's home, Martinez, after I told you *countless* times to stay far away from this, and not only that, you cracked his damn jaw! What are you not getting here?"

"Chief, you know as well as I do, he sent those flowers and he was at the office, and you know *damn* well he is gunning for Elizabeth. I'm begging you, don't take this from me." He contemplated telling Holden about his meeting with Miles and the fact that there is a good possibility they had a dirty cop on the force. But he had no evidence of that either, just the word of a CI who always expected some sort of favor in return for information.

Sympathy clouded Holden's expression but his tone was stern. "I'm afraid you've left me no other choice. You'll be on desk duty until further notice."

DANIELLE REACHED the fifth floor and stepped off the elevator walking towards the prosecutor's office. Her long coat shuffled against her legs with each stride she took.

Andrea looked up from her keyboard and through the bulletproof glass window. Danielle stood there, long red hair tucked under the front of her coat, hood hanging loosely from her head, and dark sunglasses hiding much of her identity. Hitting the intercom, Andrea asked, "Can I help you?"

Her crimson lips parted slightly. "I need to see Elizabeth Strong, please."

"Uh, please have a seat and I'll be right with you." Walking into the investigator's office, she looked perplexed.

Paul set behind his desk fiddling with something on the computer. "What's up Andrea?"

"I'm not real sure, but there's a strange woman outside asking for Elizabeth. She's wearing a long brown coat and dark sunglasses. She just looks a little odd. Maybe you should go out there and just check her out? I don't want to let her in. She's makes me a little nervous to be honest with you."

His forehead crinkled curiously. "Yeah, of course." Getting up from his desk, he walked into the main office and peeked out into the lobby. Andrea sat back at her desk while Paul opened the door enough to speak with the odd woman. "Ma'am can we help you with something?"

Turning towards him, Daniel replied, "Yes, I'm here to see Elizabeth Strong. It's very important."

Stepping further into the lobby, he allowed the door to shut behind him and placed his hand on his hip close to his gun. "Okay, well, you mind taking off your coat and having a seat? I'll check and see if she's here."

Awkwardly, she cleared her throat. "I'm sorry. I can't do that. Please, I just need to see Elizabeth Strong. Tell her Danielle DuPont needs to speak with her. I trust that she will want to hear what I have to say."

His face clouded with unease. He waved at Andrea to buzz him back in, walked back into the office, turned the corner momentarily, and demanded, "Keep an eye on her." He moved down the hall to Elizabeth's office and rapped lightly on the doorframe. "Hey Liz, there's some strange lady out in the lobby, says she needs to talk with you. She's all incognito. It's really bizarre. Says her name is Danielle DuPont?"

Closing the file she was reviewing, confusion washed over her. "Danielle DuPont? What the hell does she want?"

Shrugging his shoulders, he responded, "Hell if I know. So, you know her?"

"I mean I know *of* her. But I can't imagine what she would be doing here, to be honest." She stood up and walked past him into the hall. He followed closely behind. Pushing the door open she peeked out. "Danielle?"

Slightly turning her head to face her, Danielle said, "Elizabeth, I'm so sorry to bother you, but I really need to speak with you. Is there somewhere we can talk privately?"

A man walked into the lobby and stepped up to the

front counter. Danielle turned her body towards Elizabeth, tucking her face further under the hood of her coat as if she was hiding. "It's very important," she whispered.

Paul was still standing behind his colleague and asked, "Everything all right here?"

Shaking off her bewilderment, Elizabeth looked over her shoulder at him and said, "Yeah, yeah, it's fine. Thanks, Paul." Turning back to Danielle, she said, "I'm sorry, you kinda caught me off guard. Please, come back to my office." Showing the woman down the hall, she shut the door to her office and took a seat behind the desk, motioning for Danielle to have a seat in front of her.

Nervously, she obliged, leaving the hood over her head and glasses on her face. Elizabeth couldn't help but look at her strange. "I have to be honest, I'm wondering why you're here and what's with the get up?"

Taking a short breath, she began, "I know you don't care for me much -"

"Danielle, I hardly *know* you at all. Right now, I just want you to tell me why you're showing up at my office looking like the Unabomber and freaking everybody out?"

She pulled her bottom lip in with her teeth and released it. "I'm sorry. I didn't mean to cause any alarm I just can't risk being seen here – I need help and I didn't know where else to go."

For a brief moment, Elizabeth saw flashes of herself sitting in front of a detective saying similar words. Snapping out of it, she conceded with Danielle, "Okay. I can appreciate that, but I'm not sure what I can do for you."

Not knowing exactly where to begin, Danielle back peddled. "You know, I've always felt guilty for not coming forward six years ago."

Sitting back in her chair, Elizabeth tried to relax, anxious of where the conversation was going. "Guilt can be just as damning an emotion as any of them," she said, stopping short of feeling sorry for a woman she barely knew. "If you came here under some guise just to clear your conscience, I assure you, I don't need an apology. I'm sure you had your reasons for making the decisions you made back then and I'm certainly not one to judge." She attempted to gage the woman's sincerity but her eyes remained hidden under her dark shades.

Pulling the hood from her head, her red tipped fingers straightened the stray hairs that were rustled from the fabric. Flicking her bangs, she sucked in her stomach and fixed her posture in a grab for confidence. "You're right, and maybe I have nothing to apologize for. I just wish that when given the chance, I could have been as brave as you were. You stood up to him. I couldn't do that."

Danielle's confidence was fading quickly with Elizabeth's silence and her voice began to quiver. "And I can't help but think if I had been more like you, I wouldn't be in the current situation I'm faced with. I knew about you and I didn't care. I was just keeping my face from being on the receiving end of his fist. A lot of good that did me." She slowly pulled down her Hollywood-like sunglasses revealing the large bruise under her eye.

Elizabeth gasped and blurted out, "I see."

There was a slight embarrassment to Danielle's features. Tainted with moisture, her green eyes rose to face the object of her jealousy all those years ago. "I'm in a lot of trouble, Elizabeth, and I've put my fiancé in a really bad position because I couldn't face Steve Robinson back then. And now he is literally destroying everything I have worked so hard to build in my life." Severity took over her expression. "He came back for me. I can guarantee, he's coming for you."

ELIZABETH WAS MORE afraid now than ever before. With the reality of Steve attacking Danielle weighing heavy on her mind, she frantically drove to court looking for Martinez. *She's right, he is sure to come for me eventually. He's already begun his little cat and mouse game.* Not worried whether she would make it to Judge Bennett's courtroom on time, she breezed past security managing a quick "good morning" here and there along the way.

Remaining focused, she went straight over to Traffic thinking she may find Martinez there. One of the clerks caught a glance of her. "Good morning, Liz! You have a victim in the lobby looking for you. Real needy one there, if you know what I mean."

Without responding, Elizabeth moved quickly to the police station lobby. It was empty. Tapping on the glass to get the record clerk's attention, she asked, "Have you seen Martinez this morning?"

Refusing to look up from her computer, she replied, "Nope. But he could have got here before me."

Walking through the courthouse, he wasn't anywhere in sight. *Damn it!* She thought it was odd considering they usually they ran into each other first thing in the morning. Frustrated, she went into the courtroom and sat in her seat next to China. At least she wouldn't make the judge angry by being late. Pulling her phone from her bag, she sent Martinez a text and waited impatiently for an answer.

Looking over at her with concern, China asked, "Are you okay? What's going on with you this morning?"

She looked at her phone again before turning it over on its screen. "Angel's ghosting me and I don't know why." The nervousness came through her tone. "I *really* need to talk to him."

With a roll of her eyes, China said, "I highly doubt he's ghosting you. That's a bit extreme don't you think?"

It was extreme but it also didn't make sense why he wasn't responding to her. Managing to make it through the few cases she had, she wasted no time packing up her things as the judge started to wrap everything up. Grabbing China's attention with her haste, she barely looked at her and said, "I'm going to the detective bureau. This can't wait any longer."

Apprehension washed over her friend's face. "Are you sure you're okay? You don't look so good, Liz."

"I gotta go," she bluntly replied, surprised with herself she made it this far through the day. "I'll catch up with you later." She left the courtroom and pushed through the large door to the police lobby. Just before she reached the door to head to the bureau, Martinez emerged from the stairwell. He stopped dead in his tracks at the sight of the disappointed look on her face.

Desperation took over her voice. "I've been looking for you all morning. I really need to talk to you."

For the first time since she knew him, his expression said he didn't have time for her. Hanging his head in shame he didn't think about his words. "I'm sorry, Liz, I got your text – I – I just can't do this today. I really can't."

As he turned to go back to the stairs, he heard her yell, "Wait!" He stopped and hung his head as if it would help him listen.

"Danielle DuPont came to see me this morning."

Shaking his head, he shut his eyes before turning to look at her, defeat pouring over his face. "Holden took my badge from me, Liz. He took my badge and he took my gun. I'm on desk duty until further notice and I gotta figure out what my next move is. I'm sorry - I just - I'll call you later." Before she could respond, he turned away and disappeared behind the door and up the stairs.

A wave of shock fell over her body and her chest felt as if it was being crushed, making it hard for her to breath. He had never simply dismissed her before. She had forgotten the feeling. Managing to finally take a breath, Elizabeth straightened her purse strap around her shoulder and confidently walked out of the courthouse to her car. The dark clouds coupled with the cold mist of rain on her face solidifying her current torment.

Sitting in the driver's seat and gripping the steering wheel, her scream begged to be released. Fighting hard against the tears that were pushing from behind her eyelids, she started her vehicle and tore out of the parking lot, tires skidding against the wet cement.

On her way back to the office, her mind wandered to the past. Immediately shaking it from her thoughts, she was angry with herself for thinking this situation was remotely close to anything she dealt with before. Angel was certainly nothing like Steve. But unfortunately, she had no one else to compare him to. The fact that he told her he no longer had his badge or his gun became the new topic of worry.

Not speaking to anyone when she arrived, she went straight back to her office and shut the door. She tried to keep herself busy and her mind off of Martinez, but it was difficult. Skipping lunch, she decided to leave as soon as her letters were done. She couldn't take it anymore. She packed up her things and shut her computer down before stopping in China's office.

Peeking around the doorway, she quietly interrupted, "Hey -"

China turned around, her face lighting up, ignoring Elizabeth's vibe. "Hey! You wanna go to lunch? There's a new little Italian place and I've been dying to go!"

"Actually, I'm just letting you know, I'm going home."

Her nose crinkled. "Oh, you okay?"

"No. And right now, I just have to get out of here. I'll call you later." Disappearing around the corner, she went to the office manager. Walking into Belinda's office, she said, "Hey, Belinda, I'm sorry it's short notice but I need to take some sick time for the afternoon."

Looking at her inquisitively, she said, "Oh no, what's wrong?"

Her bottom lip quivering, she lifted her eyes attempting to hold back the tears. Taking a breath, she held it together. "I really don't want to get into it right now, but please tell Marilyn I will need to speak with her first thing tomorrow. I just need to take the rest of the day."

"Of course, Liz. Call if you need anything, okay?" She nodded her head sympathetically.

Nodding back, she wasted no time in making her exit. When she arrived home, she locked herself in and headed straight to her room. Tearing off her pants, she grabbed her comfy sweats off the chair and quickly changed. Not bothering to hang her blouse, she went to the kitchen, grabbed a bottle of wine off the shelf and opened it, pouring herself a healthy glass. Taking a large drink, she tried to calm her thoughts. She was going to need something a little stronger.

Hurt and pissed at the same time, she moved to the bathroom, opened the cabinet, and set her glass on the sink. Pulling the pill bottle from the shelf, she opened the lid, tapped one Valium into her hand, and popped it into her mouth, washing it back with a bit of Merlot.

Her sad reflection stared back at her. She didn't know what to think about Martinez and how he acted. He had never treated her like that before. Worse, she didn't know what to think about Danielle showing up at the office and everything she shared. All she knew was, she needed to get out of her own head for a minute.

Finding herself in the living room kneeling down in front of her inherited music collection, she realized she was done making an effort for the day, so she allowed the Internet radio station to shuffle songs on her phone. Grabbing a starter log, she placed it in the fireplace and threw a couple pieces of firewood on top of the rack.

Lighting the corner, she watched the flame wrap around the paper, crackling as it caught the other pieces of wood. Satisfied it would burn for a few hours at least, she settled on the corner of the sofa and pulled her mother's quilt from behind her, wrapped it around her like a long-lost hug, and took a sip from her glass before resting it in her lap.

As she stared into the flames in the fireplace, *Never Going Back Again* by Fleetwood Mac began to play. Listening intently to the song, she sang along, "Been down one time, been down two times..." She had been telling herself for years she was never going back. Never going back to being a victim; never going back to being treated like she had been. The look on Martinez' face that morning kept replaying in her mind bringing tears to her eyes as she lost herself in the music.

Hating the fact that she not only felt sorry for herself

but now she feared even more for her safety. Of all people, she never expected Martinez to brush her off the way he did. After sitting in her self-misery for a while, her phone vibrated against the table top. Taking a deep breath, she leaned over and picked it up. It was China. Hesitating for a moment, she answered it. Sniffling, she swallowed hard, "Hello."

The voice was gentle on the other end. "Heeeyyy, I thought I'd hear from you by now, sweetie. What is going *on*?"

Wiping her nose with the back of her hand she said, "Not really, but I have a fire lit and a glass of wine in my hand, so, there's that. What time is it?" She pulled her phone from her ear and saw it was nearly 5:30 pm. "I feel like I'm in a time warp and the past is slowly wrapping itself around me and there's nothing I can do about it."

"Honey, I'm sorry. Is there anything I can do?"

Setting her glass on the table, she shook her head. "Not this time. I'm not real sure anyone can do anything. Not you, not Angel - this whole day is just - I feel like I'm falling into a black hole and there's a rope there, I can see it! But when I go to grab it, try and pull myself out, someone at the other end keeps teasing me, slowly pulling it out of my reach -" She choked on the tears falling to the back of her throat. *River* by Bishop Briggs started to ring from the speakers and she couldn't hold back any longer.

China sat on the other end, waiting patiently as Elizabeth let loose an ugly cry, unsure how to comfort her friend. Feeling as if she was beginning to calm down, she asked, "Liz, what the hell happened?"

Getting up from her seat on the couch, she went to the bathroom for a tissue. "I'm just so tired of feeling like I am getting somewhere and then, *BAM*, disaster strikes me right back down."

China sighed, growing somewhat tired of the drama. "Nothing is a disaster, Liz. Now that you got all that out, are you going to tell me what is going on?"

She gasped, somewhat relieving the rapid pulse in her chest. Refusing to look at herself in the mirror fearing the monstrosity of a mascara massacre, she wound toilet paper around her hand and ripped it from the roll. Stumbling back to her corner of the sofa, she plopped down and wiped her nose again. Saving some tissue for later, she crumbled up the rest and tossed it on the table next to the bottle of wine.

Her head was hurting and her sinus cavity felt like it was packed with gauze. Her voice revealed the clogged passages when she finally shared, "Danielle DuPont came to see me first thing this morning. Steve *attacked* her. He's completely wedged himself in her life again and she swears I'm next. That's why I was so off this morning at court. When I finally saw Angel to tell him, he practically blew me off and proceeded to tell me Holden took his badge and his gun!

"He wouldn't even give me two minutes of his time to tell me why!" She took a quick breath before continuing, not allowing China to get a word in. "Not to mention the fact that he treated me like a complete piece of shit! He wouldn't even look at me, China. All he said was something like, 'I can't do this right now.' Oh, I'm sorry, *you* can't do this right now."

China's face clouded with unease. "Holden took his badge?" Shaking her head in an attempt to place some pieces together, she tried to be the voice of reason. "Okay, first of all, Martinez wouldn't just blow you off. If Holden took him off the street, there had to be a good reason, right? And I'm sure if that's the case, he's earned the right to blow off some steam. It doesn't seem personal. It's not about you, Liz. Unfortunately, it just happens to be really bad timing. Second, what the hell does Danielle DuPont have to do with anything?"

Between the wine and the crying, her voice was no more relaxed. "I can't really get into it. I need to see Marilyn first thing tomorrow. Right now, I just need to try and crawl out of this pit I've landed in."

"Liz, I don't mean to sound like your mom or anything, but how much have you had to drink?"

Pouting, she responded, "Really, China? Ugh – I'm about three glasses in. I may open another bottle. And I *might* have taken a Valium to calm down."

"I don't think it did its job, hun."

Arching her back and then bending forward, her body loosened. "I think you're right. I'm gonna need to take a nap."

Tilting her head back, her face showed a silent relief. "Good idea, honey. Get some rest and I'll see you tomorrow, okay?"

CHAPTER 11

*D*riving through downtown after leaving the prosecutor's office, Danielle tried to maintain her anonymity. She pulled into the back parking lot of the casino and snuck up the back stairs, confident no one saw her. Reaching the door to the suite, she swiped her keycard and swiftly opened the door. Quickly shutting it behind her, she fell back against it, releasing a heavy sigh. She didn't see Richard sitting on the sofa.

"Where the hell have you been," he demanded.

Flinging off her hood she screamed, "Jesus Christ, Richard!" Leaving her sunglasses on, she threw her coat across the back of the chaise. "You weren't supposed to be back until this afternoon."

Getting up he walked over to her. "Yeah, well, it didn't turn out the way I had hoped." He kissed her on the lips and then reached for her glasses. Pulling away from him, she lowered her head and slowly removed her shades. Her face was tinged with shame. Lifting her chin gently with his finger, he caught glance of the slight bruising under her eye. Anger encased his eyebrows. "You wanna tell me what happened while I was gone?"

Pursing her lips, she explained, "I'm taking care of it." Tucking her sunglasses in her bag, she strolled over to the desk to begin gathering the deposit to be taken to the bank. Sitting in the chair, she tried to ignore his glare.

Frustrated, his voice became demanding. "Dan-*ielle?*"

She stopped counting the money and threw her hands over it. "Well, there is no sense in trying to hide it. You left Saturday and Steve decided to pay a visit. But at least the weekend is over and I can get someone to cover my shift for the next few days so I can get rid of this mark on my face. So how was Atlanta?" She smirked, not attempting to hide her irritation.

Shock took over his features before enquiring, "Steve Robinson did this? Son of a bitch!" He began pacing back and forth while pushing his hand through his hair. "I knew I shouldn't have left you here alone. I'm sorry."

"Like I said, I'm handling it."

"And what, exactly, does that mean?"

"I went to see Elizabeth Strong this morning."

His eyes grew wide and his face elongated. "You - did - *what?*"

Taking in a deep breath, she tried to rub the stress from her forehead.

Trying to shake his bewilderment, he asked, "You do

realize that is the woman who accused me of not only beating my wife but trying to *kill* her?"

"You mean soon to be ex-wife?"

"You know what I mean, Danielle. Christ! Elizabeth Strong? Seriously? I just can't even begin to grasp what the hell you could have possibly been thinking!"

Snapping back, her red hair fell over her shoulder as she stood. "I was thinking, Rich-*ard*, that you left and within hours Steve's hand was making contact with my face." She cocked her head as she said, "Do you realize, in all the time I was tied to him - all those years of succumbing to his knowing what 'was best' for me, his effortless brutalities, and his disgusting way of trying to make it all seem normal -," sucking in her bottom lip, she released it and smiled, proudly declaring, "- all that time, until now, I managed to *never* be the brunt of his fist."

Riddled with guilt and anger, he asked, "So this is *my* fault? Is that what you're really trying to say?"

"No, Richard, I am not saying that at all. I am well aware this is *all* my fault. It's my fault that I didn't stand up to him years ago and it's my fault that I allowed him to continue to take advantage of me *long* after I thought I'd escaped his grasp."

She clenched her fists and gritted her teeth as she continued, "He's like a leech that latches on to your soul and begins sucking you dry. But I am telling you now, I am done being his host and I am going to do whatever is necessary to finally rid myself of Steve Robinson."

He took a breath as if to stop himself from doing or

saying something he would regret. "What did you tell Elizabeth Strong?"

"I told her enough to understand that going to her was the right thing to do. Do you have a better idea? How did your little trip go, Richard? Can Daddy Warbucks save the day this time or did you even tell him what was going on?"

Gnashing his teeth, he said, "I told you I would handle this."

Her mouth gaped as a laugh erupted from her gut. "Oh my God! You went to your dad for a loan, didn't you?" His non-response was all the response she needed. "Did you really think you could pay Steve off and make him go away?" Shaking her head, she continued, "You have absolutely no idea, do you?"

Hitting the mic on his Bluetooth, he called Smalls. "Put a hold on reviewing the weekend footage. I need you up here right now."

Not at all surprised, she rolled her eyes as her lips gathered to one corner. She sat in the chair and crossed her legs, waiting patiently for Smalls to make his entrance. Considering the security room was right below the suite, within seconds she heard the weight of his feet on the stairs.

Opening the door, he took one look at Danielle behind the desk and shook his head in disappointment. He sighed, crossed his arms over his bulging chest, and waited for Richard's instruction.

"So, Danielle has taken it upon herself, yet again, to decide what's best for this establishment, Smalls." He walked over to the bar and poured himself a decent sized glass of whiskey, shooting the liquid to the back of his throat. Giving Danielle a stern glance, he raised his chiseled chin.

Her lip curled at him in disgust. "Don't look at me like that."

After pouring himself another shot, Richard turned around, continuing with his story. "Danielle thought it was a good idea to pay a visit to our friends over at the prosecutor's office and let them in on our little problem." Taking a large swig, he raised his glass to Smalls before clearing his pathways and nodding his head as he laughed.

Interjecting, Danielle let out a slight giggle, "Yeah, well 'Boss' man thought he would get a loan from daddy and pay Steve off." Turning to Richard curiously, she asked, "I'm curious, exactly how much did you think it would take to buy him off, honey?"

Rocks glass in hand, he pointed his finger at her with a strict look on his face. "I told you I would take care of this and you didn't listen to me. My father has been in this business for years. You think he hasn't run into this type of thing before? It was going to be handled!"

Befuddled, she leaned forward on the desk, resting her forehead in her hand. Slyly moving her hand from her face, she looked at him and said, "Go ahead, Richard. You got it all planned out. Steve will gladly take your money, put it in his pocket as if you owed it to him, and still show up some time this week with his next drop as if nothing happened."

Smalls maintained his stance in front of the door. His eyes shifted from Richard to Danielle as they spoke, while he gauged the situation from their squabbling.

Richard turned to him begging, "Will you please explain this to her? My entire livelihood is at stake! We could all go to prison for Christ's sake!"

Smalls lowered and shook his head. "I don't know, Boss. Far be it from me to agree with her on anything. I really hate to say this, but I think she's right. Robinson is not just gonna walk away from a goldmine."

Danielle was almost as shocked as Richard at the response.

"Don't look so surprised, Princess." He turned to Richard and said, "I know you don't want to hear this, but getting the authorities involved at this point may be the only way any of us are getting out of this one unscathed. I think it's an option you need to consider." Focusing back on Danielle he asked, "Who did you talk to at the prosecutor's office?"

"Elizabeth Strong. She's got as much riding on this as I do." Rolling her eyes at herself she said, "Well, to a certain extent I suppose."

Running his hand through his flattop, he said, "Then I say we wait and hear what she brings back to you. In the meantime, I can bring in Lucas. Maybe he can help soften our relations with SPD since that whole debacle with Michelle."

Fear washing over her, Danielle quickly stood up and screamed, "No!"

Smalls looked at her cross.

Throwing up his hands, Richard was becoming more and more irritated. "Well, it appears the two of you have this handled." He walked over to the bar, poured another drink, and sat on the sofa.

Danielle threw a harsh glare at him. "Now is not the time to act like a petulant child, Richard!"

Rubbing the scruff on his chin, Smalls argued his case. "I personally vetted Lucas. He's a good cop."

Taking her chance at a dig, Danielle lashed out, "As good a cop as you were, Smalls?" She walked over to the bar to fix herself a drink.

His face coiled at her remark. "I worked over a pedophile who was drugging up little girls and taking advantage of them in his basement. I was never dishonest. That seems to be your game."

Growing tired of the back and forth between all of them, Richard slammed his glass on the table. "Alright, I've had enough. *Nothing* leaves this room for now. We're the only ones who know anything about this and we need to keep it that way. When Miss Strong contacts you, I'd like to know what your plan is, Danielle."

She drank from her glass and took a deep breath. "My plan is to do what I should have done six years ago."

OPENING HER EYES, Elizabeth heard a faint tapping on the glass. The wind rustled the windows. She lifted her head from pillow and tossed the throw to her side. The fire being the only light in the room, she knew it had to be past seven p.m. Touching the screen on her phone, it read 7:18. She swiped up hoping for a notification. Nothing. Martinez should have at least text her by now. Getting up from her position on the sofa, a soft tap against the window made a chill ran through her body. She walked over and placed another log on the fire hearing the sound again.

Turning her attention to the window next to the stereo, she froze. *There's no tree out front. It's not a branch.* She stood silent. A wind gust rattled the house again. Brushing off her insecurities to the pending storm outside, she took her wine glass to the kitchen to fill it. There was a tap at the window in front of her, over the sink. Peeking out the slit she made in the blind, she saw a figure move out of the way. Jolting back, wine spilled out of her glass onto her hand. Tapping on screen door to the side of the refrigerator made the glass fall from her hand, shattering in the sink. Backing away, she stared at the door, breathing heavily as her heartbeat escalated.

His voice was cool and he pleaded with her, "Lizzy, I know you're in there. Please open the door. We need to talk." Not getting an immediate response, Steve began violently banging on the door. "Lizzy! Open the door!"

Running to the living room, she grabbed her phone from the table. It was dead. *Damn it!* It only took a second for her to remember the gun.

The door shook from under his fist, and his voice over took the wind's fury. "Lizzyyyyy! Open the *fuck-ing* door!"

Dropping her phone to the floor, she sprinted to the bedroom, lifting the bed skirt as she fell to her knees. Taking in short panicked breaths she pulled out the gun case and opened it. Hand shaking, she gripped the weapon tight, steadied it with her other hand, and placed her fore-finger over the trigger guard. There was a loud shattering of glass from the door as a roll of thunder passed over the roof.

Jolting from her slumber, she flung the blanket from herself, the corner of the fabric flicking the wine glass over onto the table. Pounding on the side door inter-rupted her sigh of relief. Taking a moment to gather her waking thoughts, she told herself - *breath in... breath out...*

Again, the pounding.

"Liz, it's Martinez. Please, open the door?"

Her heart sunk and her head lowered before she pried herself from the sofa and scuffled into the dining room. Lifting her head as she exhaled, she disarmed the security system, unbolted the lock, and opened the door. "Cheese and rice, Angel! Couldn't you just send me a text?"

Covered in drizzles of rain, a drop of water slid down his forehead and seeped into his brow as his eyes begged for forgiveness. "I'm so sorry about earlier. I'm a selfish jerk."

Curling her lips at him, she pushed the handle on the screen door allowing him entry. Turning from him, her feet scuffed the carpet on her way to the kitchen to grab a paper towel and clean up the little bit of wine that spilled on the table before it left a liquid mark. She curled her feet under her legs and pulled the blanket on her lap before she grabbed the bottle, and refilled her glass.

Brushing the remaining dampness from his head, he followed her lead. He wiped off his face, took off his coat, and hung it on the back of a dining chair before joining her on the sofa. He rested the palm of his hand on her cheek and swiped under her eye with his thumb. "I really am sorry."

Slightly frowning, she was instantly embarrassed. "Oh my God. I must look a mess!"

Shaking his head as he gently rubbed her cheek, he never sounded so truthful, "You look beautiful."

She pulled away from him and looked into the fire. "I really needed you today."

Lowering his head, he took a breath before admitting, "I messed up, Liz. I haven't been completely honest with you."

Quickly turning back to him, her eyes silently begged for an explanation.

Back stepping, he was fast to correct himself. "It's not that I wasn't honest. I just didn't share everything." He rolled the stress from his shoulders and confessed, "When I first suspected Robinson sent you those flowers, I paid him a visit. I just wanted to give the guy a little warning, you know? I wasn't involved in the home visit. I stood back, out of the way, and didn't say a word."

Her face stiffened as she waited patiently for clarification.

"Well, after that asshole showed up at your office, I couldn't stand it any longer. I asked his parole officer to assist me in paying another visit. Only this time, I tried to drive the message home for him to leave you alone."

The skepticism in her face subsided.

"Turns out, things didn't go as well as I planned. He found a way to provoke me and I lost it." Shaking his head in shame, he raised it enough to look her in the eye, sucking in his bottom lip as if a silent plead for understanding.

"And that's exactly why this day is so horrible!" Setting her glass on the table, tears welled in her eyes as she bluntly stated, "Steve is laundering money through the casino."

Shocked at the response, Martinez said, "Wait - what? How do you know this?"

Taking a breath and clearing the mascara that was being washed from her face, she began to explain, "Danielle came to see me first thing this morning. At first it was really bizarre and I didn't know why she was there. I mean, she *insisted* on talking to me privately. It was almost as if she just wanted to apologize for not coming forward all those years ago. But I soon realized, how serious she was.

"He has been in contact with her since before he got out. He put her right in the middle of that whole mess with Johnny Warren, and God knows what else. After he was released, she was the first person he went to. Hell, he already had his claws in her. I always thought she was somehow involved and I guess in a way she was, but it turns out she's just afraid of him as I am. So, he pushed his way into the casino and started funneling. She never told Richard about it thinking she could handle it but now they're both in so deep she didn't know what else to do."

Martinez swept his hand through his hair, scratching the back of his head. "Wow. I guess I really messed up, didn't I?"

Steadying her breath and calming herself down she looked at him and asked, "How could you have possibly known? You just have to talk to Holden. Straighten all of this out. Right?"

Shaking his head from side to side he said, "It's not that easy Liz."

"Well, we have to do something! He attacked Danielle and it's like she said, he's going to come for me. He already has, in his own twisted little way and it's only going to get worse from here out," she pleaded with him. "She's ready to come forward, get him out of her life *and* mine, possibly for good this time."

Wringing his hands together, he was deep in thought.

"I'm afraid that isn't all."

His eyes danced around as he asked, "What more could there possibly be?"

"Well, from what Danielle said, apparently Officer Lucas has been moonlighting at the casino for some time now. She doesn't trust him and thinks he might be involved with Steve somehow. I don't know - she said she gets a bad vibe from him."

Martinez' face lit up but his head was spinning. Shaking off the information dump, he began putting it together. "Lucas is the guinea pig! Son of a bitch! Have you told anyone else about this?" Wrapping his strong hands gently around her shoulders he begged, "Liz, please tell me no one else knows about this?"

Confusion washed over her face. "No. I left the office early. I was planning on going to Marilyn tomorrow but Daniel made me promise that you were the first person I talk to. For some reason she trusts me and she knows that I trust you implicitly."

Lifting his hand from her shoulder, he tenderly touched her cheek before relaxing in his seat.

Going back to her original thought she probed, "Guinea pig? Angel, what are you talking about?"

"Remember when we went to Mansfield for the parole hearing? Well, someone screwed that up. It *had* to be someone from the inside. Those emails didn't just get lost. I've been working with my CI this whole time trying to figure out who it was but we keep coming up empty handed, bits of information here and there but nothing solid. It's all starting to make sense now. I just need the proof to connect the dots!" He pulled out his phone and started typing furiously.

"Who are you texting?"

"Holden. He needs to meet us in Marilyn's office first thing tomorrow."

 aking to her alarm, Elizabeth rolled over and smiled as she looked at Martinez sleeping peacefully. He slowly opened his eyes and smiled back at her. "Well, good morning, hermosa."

"Good morning, yourself. Are you ready for today," she asked?

"I guess we'll find out soon." He stretched his arms over his head and arched his back before pulling her into his chest and kissing her on the forehead. "Hey, do you mind if I take a shower here?"

She looked up at him lovingly, "Of course not, that's a silly question. But you don't have any clean clothes?"

"Honestly, I packed a bag and it's in the back of my car. I took a chance on you letting me stay last night. Of course, I wouldn't have blamed you if you had slammed the door in my face either." He smiled.

"Honestly, I considered it." Dragging herself from him,

she smiled back and said, "You go first. I'll put on a pot of coffee."

As the two of them took turns in her small bathroom, she smiled to herself thinking, *So, this is what it would feel like to have him around all the time. I guess that wouldn't be too bad.*

Meeting each other in the kitchen to fill their coffee cups, Martinez said, "I think it's best if we drive in separately. We don't want to bring any unwanted attention. This needs to stay between you, me, Marilyn, and Holden for right now. Did she text you back?"

After taking a sip of her coffee she said, "Yeah. I told her to meet us in the conference room. That way you don't have to come through the office and we can be more discreet. Holden meeting us?"

"Perfect. Said he'll be there at 8:15. Of course, that means we should see him around 8:30."

"I wish I could hide out for fifteen to twenty minutes. I'm sure Peggy is going to be all over my ass about leaving yesterday. I'll be lucky if I can get past her."

"Screw Peggy!"

Elizabeth laughed.

"What's so funny?"

Shaking her head embarrassed she said, "That's exactly what China would say."

"You cannot say a word to China. Liz, this is important, you have to concentrate."

Seriousness washed across her face. But then she was a tad irritated. "Angel, I'm a little nervous but I got it.

Remember, I'm the one who put him away the first time."

"You're right. And I'm sorry. I didn't forget." He threw his coat on and grabbed his night bag. Cupping her face with his hands, he kissed her hard on her lips and promised, "We're going to handle this. Together."

PULLING INTO THE PARKING GARAGE, Elizabeth started to panic as she was pulled back in time. Once again being the naïve college girl sitting in the passenger seat of her father's vehicle outside the police station, contemplating whether she had the strength to go in and tell them everything she knew. She found it ironic she was now on the other side of that fence. Pulling in a deep breath of certainty, she got out of her car and slammed the door sending an echo through the cold cement walls.

The lobby was quiet. Shaking the cold from her, she stepped onto the elevator taking it to the fifth floor. Instead of going through the back door, she walked straight to the front where she knew Andrea would buzz her right in. She waved 'good morning' and went straight to her office. Flinging her coat and bag on a chair, she sat down at her desk to pull up her docket for the morning and get ready for court. For the time being, she managed to sideline Peggy.

Hearing movement, China slithered across the hall and into an empty chair in front of Elizabeth. Her forehead crinkled with concern. "Hey! How you feeling this morning?"

Laughing at the question, Elizabeth stopped what she was doing and replied in a rude tone, "I really don't know, China. That is literally the question of the day."

Raising an eyebrow, she snapped back, "Woah, slow down, sister. You got a hang over? I have some Aspirin in my purse if you need one."

Placing her head in her hands she swept back her hair. "Wow. I'm sorry. I didn't mean to come at you like that. I just have so much going on right now."

"Liz, what the hell is going on? Did Martinez do something stupid?"

Taking a deep breath, she hesitated. It was difficult keeping her best friend in the dark. She shook her head and said, "I promise you; he didn't do anything. I really wish I could tell you, but I can't. At least not right now. There is some heavy shit going down and I'm just trying to keep it together."

Intrigue took over China's expression before it occurred to her, "Oh my God, you're like in some real-life Charlie's Angels shit, aren't you?" Excited she added, "What can I do to help?"

"Can you keep Peggy busy this morning? I'm meeting with Marilyn in a few and I need to squeeze past her."

"Well, that's not very exciting." Giving it a second thought, she said, "On the other hand, the look on her face will be priceless once she realizes she's not included! But what if she asks what's going on?"

"Tell her the truth – you have no idea. Take one of your files to her and act like you need to pick her brain about a how to handle a victim or something."

"That's kind of nauseating but I'll play along."

Sympathetically, Elizabeth said, "I know. But you would *really* be helping. I'm not sure how long it will take but I should be able to get to court on time."

Standing up, China shook her hair away from her face and said, "Okay then, let's get this party started, shall we?"

Elizabeth's lips curled with a devious smile as she watched China strut out of her office. She sat at her desk until she heard the voices coming from Peggy's office then she swiftly started down the hall. As she passed the door-way, she heard Peggy call out to her. Acting as if she didn't hear her, she let China do her part and quickly headed back to Marilyn's office, knocked on the door, and let herself in. "Good morning, Marylin."

"Hey kiddo. Are you hanging in there?" Marilyn asked.

"As much as can be expected, I guess. I just wanted to say I'm sorry for leaving so abruptly yesterday."

Grabbing her things, the two of them left through the back door and down the hall to the conference room. "It happens sometimes. I'm assuming that's what this meeting is all about?"

"I'm afraid so. Martinez and Holden should be here shortly."

As they reached the entry to the conference room, the elevator door opened for Martinez to exit. Meeting the ladies, he followed behind them.

"Good morning, Detective," said Marylin, as she sat down at the conference table and placed a legal pad and pen in front of her.

Once they were all seated and greetings were out of the way, Chief Holden arrived and walked towards the conference room spotting all of them seated at the table through the window. "Morning," he said, as he walked into the room and sat at the head of the table.

"Good morning, John. How have you been," asked Marylin.

Removing his glasses to wipe them down, he grunted and turned his eyes to Martinez. "It's been a challenge but we're maintaining. And you?"

Glancing at Elizabeth she replied, "I think I can relate."

"Enough with all the small talk," said Holden. "Tell us why we're here, Martinez. I hope it doesn't have anything to do with getting your badge back?"

"You took his *badge*," asked Marilyn.

"Another conversation for another time," Holden bluntly stated.

"Actually, Chief, now that you mention it -"

Elizabeth leaned forward in her seat and placed her hands in her lap. "Daniel DuPont came to see me yesterday. She had a lot of information to share and as you can tell, it was quite disturbing considering I left early without saying much to anyone." Taking a breath, she continued, "Not only has Steve Robinson been trying his best to torment me since he's gotten out of prison, he's now set his sights on Danielle. He attacked her this past weekend.

She also advised that he's been laundering money through the casino."

"Money laundering? Moving up in the world, I see. Even if that's true, that seems like an FBI issue to me," said Holden turning to Marylin for confirmation.

"I'm not sure that's necessarily the case," she replied.

Martinez spoke up, "Chief, I'm afraid we have a bigger issue. According to information from my CI and from what DuPont told Liz, there's an SPD cop involved."

Holden's voice matched the shock in his face, "What did you just say? You better have more than the word of a CI and a druggie-turned-casino-employee before you go accusing an SPD cop of wrong doin', son."

"Chief, you have to give me my badge back. There *is* an SPD officer working with Steve Robinson. I can't tell you who it is right now and at the moment, I don't trust anyone. But, based on the information I have, my sights are set on Lucas -"

"*Lu-cas*," Holden abruptly asked. You can't be serious? That kid couldn't fight his way out of a wet paper bag!"

"You give me the green light, let me investigate - give me access to personal files for everyone who was involved in the drug task force before it dismantled. I have a feeling Lucas was on that roster somehow. I also I have a feeling that whoever it is, be it Lucas or someone else, they've been helping Robinson for the past six years, at least. This same someone, leaked Elizabeth's involvement in trying to nail Steve back then. They were also somehow involved with everything that happened with Johnny Warren this past spring and I believe they played a part in helping get Robinson out early."

Holden remembered, "My department did agree to take Lucas in after they lost their funding. But why on earth would you peg him for this?"

"Did you know he was moonlighting at the casino," Martinez asked.

Becoming more agitated, Holden responded, "I knew he was going to school and picking up some odd jobs here and there to help pay for it. If you hadn't noticed, he's not really detective material."

Martinez became confused, then curious. "And what exactly is he going to school for?"

"He doesn't wanna be a cop. Never wanted to be a cop." Rubbing his chin, he tried to recall. "Cyber security, computer forensics maybe?"

Martinez slapped the palm of his hand to his face before wiping away his amazement and asked, "Chief, are you serious? Someone hacked my emails from Investigator McMurphy. Someone kept Elizabeth from testifying at Robinson's parole hearing."

A wave of reality crept across Holden's face before he slammed his fist on the table. "Son of a bitch!"

Pulling her pen from between her lips, Marylin responded, "It sounds to me like we should allow Martinez to look further into this. If what they're saying is true, John, it's quite possible the State could build a strong case against Robinson. As far as your officer who is allegedly involved, the FBI would definitely need to be a part of that." She twirled her pen as she thought out loud, "Give them the bad seed in your department and we get Robinson on charges of money laundering and bribery, for starters."

Holden rubbed his temples with his hand and rumbled once more. "Elizabeth, tell me everything Danielle Dupont shared with you."

"Well, after she apologized extensively for not coming forward years ago, she proceeded to tell me how Steve contacted her months before his parole hearing and asked her to give Johnny Warren a job. She thought it was just a favor until Steve asked her to bail Johnny out when he tried to run me off the road and break into my house. She said that's when she realized he had her on the hook." Looking at Chief Holden, then to Marylin, she continued, "Not surprisingly, she was able to keep all of this from Richard considering he was under investigation for conspiracy to plot his wife's murder. And she couldn't very well share any of this with him -"

Butting in, Holden asked, "Why wouldn't she tell him? From a prosecutorial standpoint, we had Richard Gardner on conspiracy to commit murder and intimidation of an employee of the State of Ohio, namely *you*, Elizabeth. All evidence pointed to him in relation to both cases. She was really willing to risk putting Gardner away to protect Steve Robinson? Sorry, doesn't wash."

Marylin spoke up. "Now come on, John, you know as well as anyone -"

"That's the thing," Elizabeth's voice permeated with

persuasion, "she claims she was going to come forward but then, everything worked out with Richard's case and she assumed with Johnny out of the picture and in jail, everything would go back to normal; Steve would still be in prison and she could forget about it. She said if things would have gone any further or Richard would have been brought up on charges, she would have definitely come forward. And I believe her."

Appearing unconvinced, Holden asked, "Okay, so what does this got to do with the price of tea in China? No offense to your friend."

She smiled. "None taken, Chief. Look, after Steve got released -"

Interjecting, Martinez said, "Mind you, with the help of an SPD officer, I'm sure of it."

"- Danielle was the first person he could contact in order for him to jump right back in the game. Really, a casino? I know it sounds cliché but come on. What better place to try and get away with anything illegal? Johnnie Warren was able to give him some background on the ins and outs of the casino and Steve already had a grasp on Danielle, so he played on that. He started making drops and giving her a cut. That way, he had even more ammunition if she decided to turn against him," said Elizabeth. "She really became concerned at her involvement when she began to suspect Lucas was in on it all. Hence, why she came to me. She didn't feel she could trust anyone else."

"Sounds very plausible," said Marylin. She turned to Holden for his reaction to the speculation.

Martinez took his chance before Holden could react. "Chief, we may not be able to get Robinson on a violation of a protection order, I get that. But that's small time considering everything else. The guys a menace and we need to get control of this situation before someone really gets hurt, be it Elizabeth, or Danielle, or someone else for that matter. Of course, he's already gone after Liz and he's attacked Danielle - He's proven he doesn't give a shit. Not only that, we have an officer representing SPD that is playing a *huge* part in this. You really want that getting out?"

Elizabeth added, "This may be nothing, but China had a date this past Friday and they went to the Volstead for a few cocktails. She said Steve showed up and they cleared the place out. Bartender claimed there was a late-night reservation. Could be a meeting place?"

"Christ," said Holden as he shook his head.

"What about Richard Gardner," Marylin asked, "What part does he play in all of this? Does he even know what's going on?"

"According to Danielle, she confessed to him a few nights ago after Tom Smalls, Richard's security guy, suspected something in viewing their security tapes. For nearly three months, it went unnoticed. This also happened to be right around the time Lucas was hired in. Of course, Richard had the brilliant idea of handling things himself and has already met with Steve. Not getting the result he wanted, she said he took off to Atlanta this weekend. That's when Steve showed up to the casino Saturday and delivered his 'warning' to her. She came to me first thing yesterday morning."

Holden took his glasses off and rubbed the inside corners of his eyes. Stretching the kink in his neck before putting his specks back on, he let out a sigh and looked at Marylin. "So, what say you, Madam Prosecutor?"

Elizabeth and Martinez glanced at each other before focusing on Marylin.

"First of all, I think Martinez is right. I'm not sure how he lost his badge, it could be of little to no consequence, but I think you two need to put your heads together and look into the personnel files like he suggested. See what you come up with. We need to get on this sooner rather than later. We also need someone to sit on the casino. I'm sorry, Detective, but it shouldn't be you. You're too recognized. Elizabeth, you as well; stay away from the casino. We can't have this getting out and see a repeat of what happened to you six years ago."

Holden scoffed, "I'm already running low on manpower. Setting up an operation like this is gonna take some time, Marylin. It's not like we can make an arrest and pull everyone in based on one drop. It could take months to get enough evidence to roll out charges on money laundering."

"I disagree. If they have video evidence of this past drop, there's more. I would assume they record everything within 500 feet of that establishment 24/7. And we can't have *any* of your men on this, with the exception of Martinez. I'm sorry, John. You understand this is entirely too sensitive." He nodded at her and she continued, "Martinez, you and Liz will need to get with Richard Gardner and Miss DuPont. Get them on the same page. I'm willing to give both of them immunity once I have more information regarding the facts of the case, *however,* that will be dependent upon their complete cooperation. Martinez, do you still have a contact with the Cleveland FBI office?"

"I do. Childhood friend of mine," he stated matter-of-factly.

"Good. We're going to need someone willing to go to bat for us in making a deal to keep Steve Robinson under our jurisdiction. I don't believe we've ever had an issue with our departments working together. They can have Lucas. But I'll be damned if I'm giving up Robinson. And if we can nail him on local *and* federal charges, all the better." Tucking her legal pad under her arm, she stood and pushed the chair in. "Well, I'll let all of you get to it. Bring me up to speed by the end of the week?"

CHAPTER 13

rriving at the station before Holden, Martinez walked into the bureau and hung his jacket on the back of his chair. With the phone stuck to his ear, Shawn raised his chin to greet him. "That sounds good. I can be there around 11:30," Shawn said finishing up his conversation.

Nodding back, Martinez sat at his desk and logged in to his computer. Pulling a piece of paper out of his coat pocket, he typed the URL into the search box taking him to the SPD personnel website allowing him access to Lucas' file.

Shawn hung up the phone. "What's up, Martinez? Any idea where Holden is?"

Coy in his response he said, "Naw, man. He's not here yet?"

He shrugged. "Haven't seen 'im."

Going back to his computer screen, Martinez didn't

offer more. Changing the subject, he asked, "You've known Lucas for a while, right?"

"Lucas? I guess so. Why?"

"No reason, really. I just heard a rumor he signed up for the detective exam."

"Actually, I think I did hear that. That guy's got grit. I believe I heard a while back his goal was to create a position for a computer crimes detective, or some shit. He doesn't make great material for a street cop but he's a wiz with computers so, he might be on to something."

"Didn't he start out at the drug task force?" He continued reading the file in front of him already knowing the answer to the question.

"Yeah. He was literally just a kid when he started. Good kid. He did a little of everything. Worked in the office quite a bit. He even transported prisoners here and there. Like I said, not really street cop quality. He just did what the rest of us did when they shut us down, take the next best thing. So, what do you got shakin' today?"

"Not a whole lot, man. Catch up on some paperwork. I'll be in and out though. I have some personal appointments throughout the day, Chief's aware." He kept his eyes on the screen trying not to make eye contact.

Standing up and sliding his arms into his coat, Shawn said, "Cool. Welp, I got some people to see. These cases don't make themselves."

Martinez minimized the window on his screen and pulled up a report he was working on before Shawn walked around the divider.

As he was leaving, Shawn offered, "It's wing night at Jimmy's. You down?"

"I don't know. One of my appointments today is the dentist. Guess that depends on how that goes, if you know what I mean."

"No worries. I totally understand. We can catch a burger this weekend."

"Awe, dude, I'd love to but I promised Liz the weekend. But I'll get with you soon. You have my word."

As he headed towards the door, Shawn said, "Alright, man." He tapped Martinez on the shoulder on his way out. "You know, you really shouldn't give a woman that much power." Smirking, he added, "But hey, whatever floats your boat."

Relieved to have the room to himself he went back to Lucas' personnel file, soaking in as much information as he could, considering Holden only permitted a 12-hour access code. After reviewing everything, he grabbed his cell phone and scrolled through his contacts. Stopping at Chico's number, he hit send. It only rang a couple times before receiving an answer.

Chico's voice permeated with excitement upon answering the call. "Como estas, hermano?"

"Que pasa, hermano! I have something you're going to be interested in. How soon do think we can put together a team?"

∼

SITTING at her desk after a full morning of chaos, Elizabeth sorted through her new cases from court. Her mind elsewhere, she didn't see Peggy standing in her door way until her knuckle knocked on the metal frame.

With her nose in the air and arms crossed, she said, "I tried to catch you this morning."

Rubbing her neck, she replied, "I had a meeting with Marylin first thing. Sorry I missed you."

"We really need to discuss some things. Mainly, the time you've been disappearing from work. It's seems like it's becoming a bad habit."

Looking down at the papers on her desk, Elizabeth sighed. "I've cleared everything with Marylin, Peggy. I'm not sure what else you want me to say. Maybe you should take your issues up with her?"

Not getting the response she wanted, she continued to pry. "I've also been thinking about this proposal of yours regarding the creation of a victim services attorney. Have you started a draft?"

Not trying to hide her irritation, she smirked and set her pen down. "I have not, Peggy. I'm really in the middle of something more important at this moment in time, while trying to keep up with my other cases. However, when I do have it ready, I will hand it over to Marylin and she can decide when to share it with you."

Pursing her lips, her voice became more dominant. "Considering I'm the Director of Victim Services, and it would essentially affect my department, I would like to be the first one to have a look at it. That way, I can let you know if there needs to be any changes or additions before you present it to her."

Even more amazed at her audacity, Elizabeth said, "Considering this is my proposal and it happens to be a position that I will literally be creating and stepping into myself, I don't think I need your help. But thanks for offering."

"I'm sure it will come across my desk at some point for approval. Keep that in mind." She flicked her hair off her shoulder as she turned and walked down the hall.

Shaking off her bewilderment, Elizabeth turned her attention to the text message that popped up on her phone.

"Things are moving quickly. Wanna meet me at Jared's for lunch?"

"PLEASE!" she responded.

"Give me ten minutes. Order me that fancy chicken wrap if you get there before me?"

Wasting no time, Elizabeth straightened out her desk, threw on her coat and snatched her bag. Stopping at China's office on her way out, she peaked in. "Hey, I'm meeting Angel at the coffee house. Want me to bring you back anything?"

Her mouth slanted to match her eyes. "No thanks. I'm actually heading out myself. When we get back, I can tell you all about my meeting with Peggy." She batted her lashes sarcastically.

"That's okay, did you just hear everything she said to me?"

China shook her head no. "I did not, I was a on call."

"Oh, just wait! Right now, I need a break," she said before waving her hand and hustling out the door.

Reaching the corner of the block, she waited for the light to turn red, allowing her to cross. The sun had managed to add some warmth to the damp air. She closed her eyes for a moment and lifted her chin to soak in a bit of much needed Vitamin D.

Giving her the energy boost she needed, she hurried to Jared's and secured a table nestled in the corner away from other patrons. By the time the waitress delivered their coffee, Martinez came through the entrance. Spotting her, he walked over and sat in the seat next to her. "Hola, mi belleza blanca."

Smiling she responded, "Hello yourself, handsome. You're in a good mood." She poured sugar into her cup and stirred it.

Raising his cup to his lips, he savored the dark Columbian blend. "It's a good day. The sun is shining, I got my badge back, and Chico and I are rolling out what might be one of the largest take-down operations seen at SPD in years."

"So, they're going to work with you guys on this?"

"So far. He spoke to his superior and they're taking it to the Deputy Director. Marylin will hopefully get a call from him before the end of the day. You manage to get a hold of DuPont?"

Before she could respond, their plates were delivered. "Just holler if you need anything else, said the waitress.

Thanking her, Elizabeth waited until she was out of earshot before continuing. "I spoke with her right after our meeting. She was going to Richard with the information and said she would get back to me. I guess this all hangs on them. I know Marylin promised immunity, but if the feds don't give them the same courtesy, I don't see it happening. Then what?"

"Is that doubt I hear in your voice, Elizabeth Strong?"

Questionably raising her eyebrows, she reminded him, "Richard Gardner may not be a sociopath, but he does have narcissistic qualities. He might not be as easy to convince as you think."

He nodded at her concern. "I get that. Honestly, I don't see there being a problem. Chico seems pretty confident. Plus, the fact that DuPont was forced into it by threat and the fact Gardner wasn't aware until recently, I have faith the feds will play nice to get what they want. Public corruption takes a front seat and if Gardner wants to save his business reputation, he'll concede."

Slouching in her chair, she placed her sandwich on the plate and wiped the crumbs from her mouth. "I have to ask, how exactly did Steve provoke you? I mean, you didn't really share any details."

Washing down a bite of his food with his coffee, he said bluntly, "He brought up my father."

A tad shocked she asked, "How on earth would he know anything about that?"

"Prisoners talk. My dad had quite the reputation in Mansfield before he went to maximum security. I'm sure after the first time I visited Robinson before he got out, he had me looked into. Husband murders wife, and kid grows up to be a cop; makes for an interesting story in the yard."

"I guess," she said as shook her head and popped a potato chip in her mouth.

"He caught me by surprise is all. Moment of weakness." Sitting back in his chair and tossing his napkin on his plate he added, "Believe me when I say, it won't happen again."

Her eyes locked with his, feeling confidence in his words.

RICHARD WALKED into the casino suite finding it quiet and empty. The dinner crowd would be coming through the doors soon. He looked around curiously and threw his keys on the desk, moving towards the door of the bedroom, which was ajar. Leaning inside, he saw Danielle half covered under the blankets. Her red hair and pale skin shimmered against the white bed clothes like she was tucked into the clouds.

Concern weighed heavy on him as he pushed aside her naked leg and sat on the side of the bed. "Hey you, you're usually up by now. You, okay?"

Her eyes refused to connect with his. Her voice more innocent than usual, she said, "Elizabeth Strong called this morning. They talked with the prosecutor and want to set up a meeting with all of us. She offered immunity for our cooperation."

A silent sigh of relief escaped him. "Well, that's a good thing, right?"

A tear rolled across her nose and onto the pillow. "None of this is good Richard. I'm so sorry," she exclaimed before burying her face.

He gently rubbed her shoulder. "Come on now, Danielle. This is not the time to lose control."

Wiping her face as she sat up, her eyes met his with sincerity. "I – am – sorry. I'm sorry for allowing him to pry his way back into my life, I'm sorry for not coming to you and not trusting you - You just had so much going on with Michelle and Cody and I didn't want to screw things up even more. I really thought I could handle it, Richard."

He swept his hand through his hair and forced a smile. "We've been through worse, right?"

She shrugged her shoulders and sniffled. "I *thought* I got rid of him. I thought after Johnny was gone, I didn't have to worry anymore. I should have known better." Her head shook in disbelief. "I changed my name for God's sake. Created a whole new identity for myself. Only for him to bully his way back into my life after I finally felt like I became something. After I met you, I didn't think he could get to me anymore. But that's what I get, I guess."

Confused but empathetic he replied, "Danielle, I've had some time to think about all of this. Although I'm still upset you didn't come to me, none of us deserve to be used and abused and taken for granted. God knows I haven't always treated people the best but I certainly didn't deserve what Michelle did to me. And I'm sorry I didn't realize it before, but babe, you don't deserve any of what that asshole did to you back then; you don't deserve it now. While I'm not sure how I feel about Elizabeth Strong, she doesn't deserve any of this either."

Her eyes fixated with conviction, "I'm going to make this right."

Squeezing her chin in a loving manner with his thumb and forefinger, he promised, "*We* are going to make it right. Michelle didn't get her way and I'll be damned if Steve Robinson is going to get his. Call Miss Strong. Let her know we're ready to meet with them."

CHAPTER 14

*A*rriving to the bureau earlier than usual, Martinez began organizing himself for the day. He waited for Holden to get through his morning routine before knocking on the door.

Looking up over his glasses while blowing on the hot liquid in his cup he said, "What do you got, Martinez?"

His face was lit with enthusiasm. "Morning, Chief. Notice I waited until you had your second cup before coming in?"

Unimpressed, he looked down at the newspaper and replied, "Notice how I just *started* my second cup?"

Unsure how to respond, Martinez was puzzled. "I thought you said -"

He set the paper down on his desk. "Come on Martinez, I'm just yankin' your chain. To be honest, I'm not happy with anything that's going on right now and frankly, the fact that it's been happening on my watch is a slap in my face. But I have to say, I'm damn proud of you. Now tell me what you got."

Grabbing his notepad from his pocket, he focused. "Right." He sat in one of the chairs in front of the Chief's desk. "Elizabeth has us set to meet with Richard Gardner and Danielle DuPont later today after business hours considering everyone's need to be discreet. Chico, who already has the go ahead from the AG's office, and Marylin will question them separately. If they're satisfied, they'll make their offers. If everyone agrees to move forward, we'll take over and review all the details for their first meeting with Robinson."

"Sounds like a solid plan. What did you find out about Lucas?"

"Everything I read in his file leads to Robinson in some way, shape, or form. He started at the drug task force about six years ago, which is well within the time frame when someone sold Liz out and squashed the drug trafficking case against Robinson. Lucas was pretty young at the time, making him impressionable. He helped transport prisoners on occasion and I believe he still does, which means ample and personal access to inmates, including Robinson. I'm waiting on transport records for Robinson to and from court, etc. Also waiting on phone and visitor records from Mansfield."

He looked down at his notes for a moment to refresh his train of thought. "Uh, he mostly did office admin back then and has been attending college classes off and on for the past six years, specializing in computer forensics and cyber-crime, giving him the know-how to hack emails, websites, enter protected servers – and remain a ghost the entire time. Let's see, *and* right about the time Robinson gets paroled, Lucas begins moonlighting at the casino. But the real kicker is, Johnny Warren was a high school class-mate of his." He swatted his hand with his notepad. "I'm telling you, he's our corrupt cop. He's quiet, stays to himself, and plays dumb more than I care to deal with. There's also a rumor he's geared to take the detective exam. The higher up one crawls, the less likely he is to be noticed."

Holden's expression suggested he was on information over-load. He took in a deep breath and grunted as he exhaled through his lips. "You give all of this to Reyes?"

Shaking his head in the affirmative he said, "He agrees. We're meeting with Tom Smalls to gather video evidence from the previous drops, see what else we can find linking him."

"Good work, Martinez. The feds just love when you do everything for them." He rolled his eyes. "When and where do we meet with Gardner?"

A LARGE BLACK sedan with heavily tinted windows pulled into the parking garage, stopping in front of the large door leading into the county building. Richard exited and looked around before grabbing Danielle's hand and helping her out of the vehicle, her black coat blending with the shadows. Marylin was waiting for them just inside. She swiped her keycard allowing them entry into the main lobby.

Once inside, she turned to Richard acknowledging him. "Mr. Gardner." Putting out her hand to Danielle she said, "Miss DuPont, it's nice to meet you. I'm Marylin Bennett. Unfortunately, Richard and I are already familiar with each other. But I want to thank you both for coming." Directing them to the stairwell door, she led them to a large conference room past the break area.

"I believe you both know Elizabeth Strong." Pointing to Chico Reyes she said, "And this is Investigator Francisco Reyes with the FBI field office in Cleveland. He's here on behalf of the U.S. Attorney's Office." She motioned to the chairs. "Shall we?" Once everyone sat down, Marilyn continued. "So, we all know why we're here, right? Miss DuPont, you shared some information with Miss Strong and now the involvement of the FBI has come into play due to the severe nature of the circumstances."

Danielle gripped Richard's hand as if her life depended on it. Her confidence was fading quickly.

Although the air began to feel tense, Marylin could sense it. "However, that being said," she turned to Danielle, "we are going to get this guy. Now, this isn't going to be easy, but together we can do this. You will have all the support you need." She looked at Elizabeth and back to Danielle. "Now I know you trust Elizabeth, that's why you went to her. I just want you to know, you can trust me too. So, Investigator Reyes and I are going to ask you some questions and some of them may be uncomfortable, but we have to ask them, okay?"

Danielle nervously looked to Richard and to Elizabeth and then Chico before going back to Marylin again. Her heart rate accelerated as her head spun.

Taking her cue, Elizabeth caught Danielle's eyes. She stood from her seat and soothingly grabbed hold of the other woman's arm. Glaring into her pupils, she swore to her, "You – got – this."

As the uncertainty slowly left Danielle's face, Elizabeth softened her grip and walked out of the room shutting the door behind her. Moving to the break room next door, she stood in front of the coffee machine contemplating the choices. Settling on espresso, she grabbed her small cup and made herself comfortable at a round table.

She scrolled through her phone while she waited for Marylin and Chico to finish their questioning. Sipping on her second cup of espresso, she heard footsteps and hollow voices coming from the stairwell. Martinez came around the corner into the breakroom and Holden followed right behind him.

Looking up from her phone, she forced a smile. "Hey, you."

"Hey, yourself," said Martinez.

Holden nodded his head at her, pulled his wallet out of

his back pocket, and placed a dollar into the vending machine.

"Have they been in there a while?"

Now that she had someone to pass the time with, Elizabeth put her phone in her bag. "Maybe an hour or so?" Shrugging her shoulders, she said, "They've got a lot to talk about."

As soon as Martinez pulled out a chair to sit down, they heard the conference room door open. Marylin walked in and looked around the breakroom at everyone. "Okay, I think we've got something solid and ready to get this rolling. Would you all join us, please?"

They filed into the conference room taking a seat in the empty chairs surrounding the table. Richard and Danielle squeezed each other's hand and gave a glance of support.

Placing his hands through his hair in an attempt to brush away the stress and after an awkward moment of silence, Richard spoke up. "So, right now, if I don't agree to this, my casino is already pegged. You'll continue on with your investigation regardless. I mean, basically I'm damned if I do and damned if I don't."

Chico sat there, calm as a cucumber and looked into Richards eyes. "Not really. You're getting immunity. The AG's office is getting the papers ready for you to sign as long as you cooperate. *And* you're able to be at the helm of the ship to avoid a public relations nightmare. I'm not sure what more you could ask for."

Butting in Holden asked, "I thought we were past this?

Why the hell did you call us in here if you're not ready to get down to the nitty gritty?"

Chico apologized. "I'm sorry, Chief Holden. Martinez, why don't you lay it down for Gardner?" He winked and as he smiled, his chubby cheek revealed a deep dimple.

Taking his shot, Martinez said, "This is it, Richard. Do you want to be indebted to Steve Robinson or whoever they happen to send your way, or do you want steer the situation in a direction that helps you? It will only look better on you if you're working with the authorities from the moment you knew what was going on. That means that your establishment was the one to notice corrupt activity and decided to act upon it."

Richard shook his head positively. "As long as I have a guarantee that Danielle and I are safe from prosecution, we'll do whatever you need us to." Reaching her eyes with assurance, he gripped her hand a little tighter.

Marylin tapped the end of her pen on the table. "Okay, now that that's settled, Martinez and Investigator Reyes, I'll let you take it from here."

Chico nodded his head at Martinez giving him the floor. Turning to Danielle and Richard, Martinez said, "The first thing we have to do is set up a meeting with Robinson. Let him know you've had a change of heart due to recent events. Give him the idea he has the upper hand to a certain extent. You following me?"

Richard nodded.

"Okay, he thinks you're the rich kid from across the tracks that would do anything to fit in with his crowd and do anything to avoid pissing that crowd off. Danielle, unfortunately you're still the young, naïve, street trash trying to get ahead."

She threw him a dirty look.

Martinez threw up his hand defending himself, "*I'm* not saying you are street trash, but Robinson *thinks* you are and you need to play on that. Richard, you need to act like you're in control of your woman, so to speak. Make him believe that she's *your* property now, not his. We all know this isn't who you are but you have to pretend to be the people he *thinks* you are. The fact that Richard is leading this whole conversation will make it a little easier. After all, it is your casino and he is making a deal with you."

Chico added, "We need you to begin the conversation with what he offered you last time. Get him to repeat as much as you can like your negotiating all over and act as normal as possible. Danielle, you will be there, but only to act like the obedient fiancé, understand? The two of you want to portray that as much as you can. Richard, you didn't give in to Robinson the first time because you felt your hand was forced by Danielle; you should have been the one to make the decision, if that makes sense."

Richard rolled his neck at Danielle and said, "Well that shouldn't be too difficult." She turned away from him rolling her eyes in the process.

Martinez attempted to get past the tension forming in the room. "Look, this isn't going to be easy for anyone but you have to remain focused. Robinson cannot get the idea that he's being recorded. I have a feeling that he's going to buy it if you sell it properly. Once he agrees to working with you, even if it's just a small percentage at first, you make it official. Don't act like your too greedy. You just want to build the relationship. You'll need to know the ins and outs including who is making the drop and when. I believe he will be open to your having inside information as long as he knows you're in it to win it."

Richard shook his head in agreement, indicating he understood. "It seems like they've been making drops on our busiest night, Saturday. Around one to two am is the sweet spot, according to what Smalls has seen in the video footage."

Martinez confirmed it. "He emailed me the files. If you can set up a meeting with Robinson in the next day or so, we can have a team set up for the drop this Saturday."

DANIELLE SAT on the plush sofa with her hands nervously wrapped around a rocks glass as she waited for Steve to show up to the suite. She stood up, took a sip of her scotch, and began pacing the floor.

From his desk, Richard was keeping an eye on the cameras outside. Calling down to Smalls in the security room he asked, "Smalls, are we clear?"

"Yeah, Boss. It's just me."

"Good. Let me know as soon as you see his vehicle enter the parking lot. And make sure you have a camera with good range on the back door." Focusing on Danielle he said to her, "Could you just relax? You're making me nervous. Have a seat and enjoy your drink, will you please?"

Irritation shadowed Smalls' response, "Everything is set, Boss. You just worry about what's happening up there." Scanning the screens across the security room, he stopped at the one focused on main entrance, spotting Steve's white four-door. His eyes moved from camera to camera, following the vehicle to the back of the casino. "He's here, Boss."

Richard switched to the camera revealing the back door that led to the suite stairwell. He watched as Big D and Steve exited the driver's side of the car. Lucas greeted them offering a handshake and led Steve through the entrance. Smalls met him at the bottom of the stairs.

Grinning at Smalls and pulling on his jacket lapel, Steve said, "Looks like we might be working together after all."

Chin up and chest bowed, Smalls refused to respond. Reaching the top of the stairs he swiped his keycard and the two men entered the suite.

Standing from his chair Richard said, "Mr. Robinson, thank you for coming."

"Honestly, I didn't think I would hear from you but, I take it you got my warning?" His eyes shot to Danielle who remained seated, timidly sipping on her drink.

Silently offering the seat in front of him, Richard sat back in his chair with confidence. "You call it a warning, I call it desperation, but we're not here to contemplate your strategy. That being said, I would like this meeting to fair better than our first. Of course, had you approached me to begin with, we could have had this worked out already. However, from here on out, I am the only one you'll be dealing with. Of course, with the exception of Smalls. Danielle, or Jenny as you like to insist on calling her, she is no longer of your concern. She's mine and you will forget her name from here on out. Got it?"

Steve sat across the desk moving his head slowly up and down. "All right. I can dig that." He placed his hand on his knee and relaxed his stance, "I had a feeling you'd come around."

Richard looked at Danielle and demanded, "Make yourself useful and get the man a drink." Turning back to Steve he said, "I think we can get on the same page. There is just entirely too much money to be made."

A smile stretched across Steve's thin lips. "That's what I'm talking about."

Richard quickly went back to the task at hand. "Good. Going back to your original offer -"

Danielle placed a tumbler of scotch on the desk in front of Steve and his eyes followed her briefly before turning back to Richard. "Now see, I'm afraid that offer is no longer on the table."

Attempting to redeem himself, Richard explained, "Don't get me wrong, ten percent is quite generous, considering. But we can't forget that I'm the one taking all the risk. If we're going to be in business together, I think it's only fair. This type of operation is going to require a little more than your man stopping by on a Saturday to play a little black jack filtering hundreds of thousands of dollars. I've got books to cook for my cut, personal security that needs to be hired -"

Propping his foot on his knee Steve boldly stated, "I've got some boys in blue that would be happy to help with that."

A smile formed around the whites of Richard's teeth. "Perfect! There are many details that need to be worked out. I think fifteen percent of everything you bring in is quite fair, indeed. I also need a heads up on the drop schedule and who to expect. If you want me to play ball, I have to be an actual part of the team."

Steve tilted his head and chewed on the inside of his bottom lip. He nodded slowly and said, "Seems you've given this some thought. Remember, I have people I answer to as well. My guy loses me damn near twenty percent to clean it on your tables. As you know, the House always wins. If we wanna get technical, you're the one making out here." He pondered for a moment. "I think to start out, ten percent is all I can do. Once we get rolling and begin to trust each other a bit more, my people may be willing to increase your share of the pot. Who knows?"

Richard glanced at Smalls who signaled at him to accept the offer. "All right, Mr. Robinson. I think you have yourself a deal."

Steve stood and washed down the shot in his glass. He pulled a mobile phone from his pocket and slid it across the desk at Richard. "This is the only form of communication you will use for me. My guy will be here Saturday." As he started to walk out, he glanced at Danielle one last time before turning to Richard, "Glad we could work this out. I'll be in touch."

CHAPTER 15

*M*artinez tapped on his phone screen. It was just past ten o'clock pm. Looking around the room at his team he said, "Alright, everyone understands their positions and what to look out for? We've got all the exits to the casino covered and two men sitting on Volstead, since we determined Robinson's girlfriend works there as a bartender and it's where he hangs out on the weekends. We keep in communication at all times. Reyes and his partner will be in plain clothes inside Chip's posing as drinking and gambling customers, keeping an eye out for the actual drop."

Chico nodded at his friend and took over. "You've all been sent pictures of the money man, Robinson, his vehicle, and his drivers. Myself and Agent Jackson will follow the target out of the building once the transaction is complete and only after he exits the establishment, do we make our move. We take them all down as soon as he attempts to enter the vehicle at the pick-up location. Although they've been creatures of habit so far, that could change and we all need to be on top of our game. We get one shot at this. Does anyone have any questions?" He looked around the room at his team dressed in black with white FBI letters on their jackets, slightly revealing the bullet-proof vests underneath. "Alright. Let's do this."

SITTING on the sofa with a glass of red wine in her hand Elizabeth gazed into the fire place, losing herself in the flames and the vinyl playing in the background. Her choice of albums for the evening was lined up for the next hour or more. She was nervous as is but the music helped her keep her mind off things, to an extent. Her phone vibrated against the coffee table. It was China. Smiling she swiped the screen and answered. "Hey you."

"Hey yourself. What are you up to?"

"Oh. you know, a fire, a glass of wine, music. My regular go-to. I opted against a warm bath." She giggled slightly. Pulling her phone from her ear, she looked at the time and asked, "What are you up to? How did your date go?"

Sighing on the other end, China admitted, "Obviously not so well if I'm talking to you. That's a whole other story. I just wanted to check in. Make sure you're doing okay. I know you have a lot on your plate right now."

Shaking her head as if China could see her, she replied,

"I'm just trying to practice a little self-care and get this night over with to be honest. I just hope come tomorrow morning, I can get a little relief. I know I've been distant and I promise I will share everything with you soon."

With an enthusiastic voice she said, "Liz, it's okay. I get it. It just sucks a little that I'm your best friend and have no idea what is going on with you. I just want to help."

"I know. And it totally sucks not being able to share, trust me. But I promise, after tonight, I'll tell you everything."

"I'm gonna hold you to that. So, you better call me for coffee first thing in the morning. I want all the details!"

Smiling over the phone she said, "It's a date."

"Okay, well, I need get out of these clothes and pour myself a nightcap. I love you!"

"I love you!"

MARTINEZ SAT in his vehicle at a good distance from the entrance of the casino but far enough away to go unnoticed in the shadows. His position gave him eyes on all vehicles coming and going as well as people entering and exiting the casino. He pulled a water bottle out of the cooler from the back seat. As soon as he opened the cap and took a drink, he spotted Steve's car. Radioing the team, he said, "Robinson's vehicle just entered the perimeter; white, four-door BMW, tinted windows. Stand by." He watched as the vehicle dropped off the money man and crept off to a private parking spot not far from the entrance.

Sitting at one of the bars by himself, Chico sipped on a tonic with lime. He fit in perfectly as the lonely middle-aged man looking for some action on a Saturday night. Keeping an eye on the target, he pulled out his phone and began to scroll, remaining inconspicuous. Witnessing the target trade a briefcase of money for chips and then join a poker table, he updated his team. "Gonna be a little bit. He just joined a Texas hold'em table."

Martinez laughed and responded, "He's been going for the quick losses. Black Jack, Roullette. They're gonna make us work for it this time."

Acting as if he was talking on the phone and checking out a pretty lady, Chico winked at her as he said to Martinez, "Hell, I got all night, hermano."

"Yeah well, personally I'd like to get this over with and be with mi mujer." As soon as he said it, he regretted it.

The heckling from his team came through the radio, once the translation of 'mi mujer' was revealed. Each man sharing a childish joke of his own and inferring Martinez was 'whipped'.

One man chimed in after searching for the definition on his phone, "So, I'm confused, is the translation, my wife or my woman?"

Someone else chimed in, "Does it matter? Martinez got the fever, man. *That* shit will kill you. Just ask my cousin."

"Don't hate!" Martinez couldn't help but laugh at some

of the things they flung at him. "Alright, alright. Get back to work."

Everyone held steady in their positions for nearly two hours sharing goofy tidbits with each other. After going quiet from the conversation for some time, Chico's voice came through the radio, "Guys, guys, target is packing up, getting ready to cash out. Everyone in position."

The radio went eerily still.

"Target is on the move. Headed towards the main entrance." Finishing the last sip of his drink, Chico threw a five-dollar bill on the bar and headed out behind the man. Nearing the exit, Chico saw the white vehicle pull up to the door. With the man several feet away, he yelled over the radio, "Go, go, go!"

Within seconds a black SUV and sedan blocked the vehicle in the driveway as another black vehicle squealed its tires coming around the corner from the back of the building. Red and blue lights began to flash, attracting the attention of others and drawing them out to the parking lot. Eight men with guns pulled surrounded the vehicle while Chico grabbed the man with the briefcase from behind, slamming him onto the car. "Como va su dia, amigo," he asked as he yanked the briefcase from the man and slapped handcuffs onto him.

Pointing his gun at the back passenger side door, Martinez yelled, "Open the door and step out slowly!"

Another agent had his weapon on the driver and secured him as soon as he stepped out of the vehicle. Big

D's lips puckered as he said, "There's no one else in the car, my man."

Keeping his weapon raised, Martinez slowly opened the vehicle door with his left hand. The back seat was empty. Lowering his gun and looking around in disgust, Martinez noticed Lucas standing off in the corner texting on his phone. He walked over to him and asked, "Who you texting there, Lucas?"

He looked up for a moment. "Buddy of mine. Pft, he is not going to believe this!"

Putting his hand out Martinez demanded, "I'm gonna need your phone, Lucas."

He caught his eyes with defiance. "What?"

"Your phone, Lucas," Martinez demanded.

Grimacing he replied, "Get the hell outta here, Martinez. You're kidding with me, right? Is this some kind of test for the detective exam?"

"Lucas, we're gonna need you to come down to the station and have a little chat. If you don't want to give me your phone, I'll get a warrant and the judge will grant it. It'll be better for you to cooperate."

His face reflecting the seriousness of the situation, he handed over his phone voluntarily and Martinez stuffed it into his pocket. "Come with me." Speaking to the two men sitting on the Volstead bar, he radioed in, "What's happening downtown?"

The man behind the wheel of the van down the street said, "Haven't seen movement since we got here. Quiet as a church mouse."

"Shit!" Frustrated, he allowed the other officers to handle the driver and the money man while Martinez put Lucas in his vehicle and drove to the station. Pulling into the roundabout, he parked in front of the station doors and led Lucas to the interview room off of the lobby and slammed the door behind them. Refusing to sit, he gripped the back of the steel chair in front of him and glared at Lucas. "You need to tell me where Steve Robinson is."

His demeanor was beginning to show signs of fear. "Look man, I don't know what the hell is going on but -"

"Save it Lucas. You're Robinson's right-hand man. I can't believe it took me this long to figure it out."

"Whoa, whoa, whoaaa! Robinson's *man?* What the hell, Martinez?"

"That's right. We know everything and we're going to prove it. Six years ago, at the drug task force, you started informing him about Liz when she tried to turn him in for drug trafficking, you helped target her with Johnny Warren when she wouldn't do what you wanted, you hacked my emails so she couldn't show up at Robinson's parole hearing, and now you've embedded yourself so far deep into his shit, you're going to go down for money laundering. The feds are all over this, as you can see, and I need to know where Robinson is - *now*!"

Lucas' mind was swirling around the room. "Dude, I have – *no* – idea what the hell you are talking about!"

The metal chair made a horrid sound against the floor as Martinez pushed it into the side of the table growing more impatient by the second. "How exactly did you land the job at Chip's?"

~

THE ALBUM *MORRISON Hotel* by the Doors dropped on the turntable and *Road House Blues* began to play, putting Elizabeth in a flirty mood. She stood up and danced around the table knowing that after tonight, she wouldn't have to look over her shoulder any more. And neither would Danielle.

There was a short pause before the next track began to play. Hearing a car pull into the driveway diverted her attention. She wasn't expecting anyone. She was only waiting for a text from Martinez letting her know what was going on. She tapped the screen of her phone to see it was 1:30 am. Peeking out the blinds of the side door, she saw Shawn Johnson staring out at the lake, waiting for her to answer.

Turning off the alarm and unbolting the lock, she partially opened the door. "Detective Johnson?"

He turned to her with a large smile on his face. "Hey Elizabeth, how you doing?"

"I'm okay, I guess. I don't mean to sound rude but, what are you doing here?"

"I know it's late, but Martinez asked me to check on you. I'm afraid I have some bad news."

Instantly insecure she asked, "Oh my gosh seriously?"

His face was expressionless. "Apparently there's an

APB out on Robinson. Something went down at the casino and they made a few arrests. I guess Robinson is involved somehow and they can't find him. Martinez was worried about you so he had me come out." The lake breeze caught his ear through the porch screen before he asked, "It's kind of cold. You're not gonna make me sit out here and wait till Martinez gets here, are you?"

She looked around nervously but felt reassured by his presence. Embarrassed at herself for questioning him, she was glad he was there. "I'm so sorry! Please, come on in. I have some coffee already made. It's not fresh but I'm sure it's still good." Allowing him to enter, she shut the door behind him. "Of course, I have wine too but I guess you're on duty, huh?"

Looking around he replied, "Coffee is fine. Thank you."

Elizabeth started towards the kitchen and spoke so he could hear her. "I guess Angel finally filled you in on what was going on?"

Making his way to the living room, he glanced at the fire and the glass of wine on the table. "You could say that. I heard quite a bit on my scanner. I know they arrested Robinson's driver and some other guy with him. They thought Robinson would be in the vehicle. Something about laundering money? Martinez took Officer Lucas to the station to question him. I guess he was there when it went down. They're probably going to be with him for a while."

Brushing it off she replied, "I guess that makes sense.

I'm really glad he asked you to come. Of course, I thought it would be a quiet evening and after tonight, I wouldn't have to worry. So much for that!" Pausing for a brief moment, reality hit her. "Do they have *any* idea where Steve might be?"

He looked around the house scoping things out. "I take it you got the low down on whatever's going on?"

She opened the cabinet, pulling a mug from the shelf. "I was actually the first to know. I brought it to Angel. It's kind of a long story."

Shawn walked over to the stereo turning the volume up excessively. Elizabeth finished pouring the coffee and placed the carafe back onto the pot's burner. She slowly walked to the entry of the dining room, holding the hot cup with both hands as he inched towards her. "What are you doing," she asked.

LUCAS PULLED out the chair in front of him and sat down. Leaning his elbows on the table he cradled his shaking head with his hands. "Oh my God." He looked up with sincerity and begged with Martinez, "Man, I don't know what the hell is going on, seriously. I – I needed a steady second job to pay for school, man. I'm almost ready to graduate! Johnson told me I would be a shoe-in at the casino. Especially since Gardner's top security guy used to be SPD. I was sold when he said it paid really well!"

Taken aback, Martinez begged for confirmation.

"Johnson? Detective Shawn Johnson told you about the job at Chip's?" His mind reeled and began to piece together all the evidence he originally missed. *Johnson was undercover at the drug task force for years. Johnson was the one who screwed up his email about the parole hearing, sending it to the wrong recipient.* One of the last conversations they had replayed in his head verbatim...

"I didn't take you for a moonlighting kind of guy."

"Yeah, me neither but early retirement comes at a cost."

Martinez slammed the chair into the table again. "Son – of – a – bitch!" Pulling out his phone, he hit Liz's contact.

Leaning on the dining room chair in front of him, Shawn cocked his head and crossed his fingers together, curling his lips at Elizabeth in disgust. "You have been a thorn in my side since the first time I heard your name -"

Elizabeth's heart began to thump beneath her breasts. Her grip on the coffee cup became more pronounced and she took a deep breath through her nose without changing the stone expression on her face. Unable to move, she felt the weight of the slippers on her feet as if they'd turned to cement.

"- I *told* Steve you were going to continue to be a problem but he just wouldn't listen to me. Lucky for you, he wouldn't agree to how I originally suggested handling you. Of course, now it's a moot point. Threatening you didn't work, running you off the road didn't work." Letting out a disturbing laugh, he admitted, "Hell, I even tried to get you fired with that whole Brandon DeFranco debacle."

The corners of her eyebrows pulled towards her nose in wonder.

He proudly stated, "Yeah, from what I hear it only resulted in you receiving a reprimand of sorts. In all honesty, Elizabeth, after your parent's accident six years ago, we thought for sure you would get the message and we would never hear from you again."

A tear streamed down her cheek and for a moment Shawn preyed on her weakness. "That's right. In Steve's original plan, you were supposed to be in the car. But I think the good-girl tragedy it turned out to be, gave the story the little extra drama it needed. Hell, I thought after losing her parents, and after having been through such a traumatic trial, no more Elizabeth Strong! But here we are." He stood up, his back cracking as he straightened it.

Unsure of whether the lump in her throat was about to unleash an ugly cry, or if she was about to vomit, the bass from the music thrashed her eardrums. The song *Peace Frog* began playing, the lyrics spinning her mind out of control -

- There's blood in the streets
it's up to my ankles,
There's blood in the streets

it's up to my knees –

ENTERING FIGHT OR FLIGHT MODE, Elizabeth gained her composure and glanced behind Shawn, noticing her phone light up on the coffee table. There was no way to get past him. Quickly gaining control of her thoughts, she gripped the handle of the coffee cup and flung the hot liquid across the table into his face and bolted to her bedroom. She slammed the door behind her and secured the lock. Her back against the door, she leaned over attempting to catch her breath.

"God – *damn* – it!" screeched Shawn as he swiped his hand down his face and flicked the brown liquid from his fingers in anger. Slowly walking around the table, he reached the door she fled through. Resting his head against it, he knocked lightly. "Liz, open the door and this doesn't get ugly. Come on out. It's time for us to take a little trip."

Falling to the floor on her knees, she lifted the bed-skirt and pulled out the gun case. Fumbling at first to open it, she grabbed the gun from its storage and crawled around to the other side of the bed for cover. Steadying her hands on the mattress, she directed her target to the door and wrapped her fingers around the grip placing her forefinger over the trigger. Her heart thumping, she feared she would pull it prematurely.

∿

ORDERING LUCAS INTO HIS VEHICLE, Martinez sped out of the station parking lot, placing his light on top of his vehicle. His voice was calm, yet urgent over the police radio. "This is Detective Angel Martinez; I need an all-points bulletin on Detective Shawn Johnson. Officers in need of immediate assistance at 210 Cedar Lane. I *repeat! Officers need immediate assistance at 210 Cedar Lane!*"

~

GROWING IMPATIENT, Shawn pulled his gun from its holster. Tapping the heavy, steel barrel on the hollow, wooden door he said, "Liz, you got nowhere to go and we're running out of time."

Her elbows were locked and her finger brushed the trigger, waiting.

Backing away from the door Shawn lifted his leg, pulled back, and planted the bottom of his boot above the doorknob. The door forcefully flung open, splintering the wood on either side.

Without hesitation Elizabeth pulled the trigger, the bullet burying in his right shoulder. The sound was deafening. She pulled the trigger again.

Grabbing his shoulder, he fell back, landing on the dining room chair just outside the bedroom door, before he fell to the floor, his weapon discharging from the blow. His face, overcome with disbelief.

Elizabeth's eyes became saturated and she struggled to breathe. The heavy piece of metal relaxed in her hand and fell against the comforter. Squinting her eyes shut, she twisted her neck and tried to shake the ringing from her ears. As she opened her eyes, red and blue angels drifted around her before everything turned black.

~

BATTING HER LASHES, she came to. "Hola, bella," said Martinez as he brushed her brow with his thumb and smiled. "I knew you were a decent shot."

Realizing she was in a hospital bed she panicked. "Oh my God, where's Shawn? Did you find Steve? What about Danielle?" A sharp pain in her side made her wince.

"Hey, hey! It's okay. Lay back, Liz. You're being treated for trauma. Johnson was able to let off a round after you shot him. Unfortunately, you were in the path of the ricochet. Don't worry, the bullet went right through and it didn't hit any major organs. You're gonna be okay. You passed out and were dehydrated from the wine. Not to mention, you shot someone, for Christ's sake. You'll be able to go home soon, I promise. Johnson is here at the hospital and in police custody. He'll be fine. At least until a jury gets a hold of him."

She entertained his enthusiasm by mimicking it and allowed herself to relax, laying her head back on the pillow.

"And Robinson is in custody. He was at the Volstead the whole time. His little girlfriend was having a private party for him upstairs. Turns out, Katrina has an apartment in the same building. As for Johnson, he was staking out the casino and saw the arrests go down. He knew the walls were shaking. He was desperate and took it out on you. No one had clue." He brushed her hair off her forehead.

Her eyes begged, "Just tell me we got 'em."

"We got 'em. Liz. You guys really got him this time."

CHAPTER 16

wo weeks later...

ELIZABETH PULLED into an open spot in the parking garage, leaving the vehicle run while she attempted to gain the courage to go into the office. She didn't think her first day back would be so difficult. Taking a deep breath, she closed her eyes for a moment. Hearing a vehicle pull in next to her, her eyes slowly opened meeting China's smiling face in the car next to her.

Motioning for Elizabeth to join her, China proceeded to enjoy the remainder of her cigarette. After her friend jumped into the passenger seat and shut the door, she said, "Hey, good morning! Ready for your first day back?"

Pulling the lighter and pack of cigarettes from the console, Elizabeth opened the top and grabbed a smoke from the pack, placing it to her lips to ignite it. As she exhaled and cracked the window, she replied, "I'm just not ready to face everyone fawning over me and asking me how I'm doing."

Waving her French-manicured fingernails through the air, China told her, "Oh please! You're a hero around here now, Liz. You did a good thing and that should never go unnoticed. And you studying for the bar is the talk of the office. You should be proud. Everyone else is." She winked.

A tad embarrassed, Elizabeth said, "Well that didn't take long." Shaking her head she took a drag from her cigarette.

"You've been gone two weeks! Marilyn actually waited to make the announcement until last Monday. And don't worry, everyone knows you're only here until noon today just to get everything in order. Go to your office, shut the door, and no one will bug you, not *even* Peggy." She arrogantly cocked her head and batted her eyes as if a battle had been won.

"Wow, I'm impressed!" Elizabeth flung her butt out the two-inch crack and pushed the lever to close the window. "Okay, well, as you always say, let's get this party started, shall we?"

Reaching the fifth floor they walked to the back door and China punched the code to enter. As soon as Elizabeth walked through the threshold of the main office, there stood the entire office team clapping their hands loudly. Mildred immediately ran to her and embraced her in a hug. "Welcome back," she screamed.

Elizabeth winced as she said, "Thank you Mildred, but you're hurting me."

Backing away she palmed her mouth with her hand. "Oh my gosh, I'm so sorry. Are you still in pain?"

Elizabeth's eyes were forgiving. "It's okay, just a little tender yet. But healing nicely."

Mildred gently cupped Elizabeth's face with both her hands and said, "You should be proud, Elizabeth." Shaking her head back and forth as if to keep her from tearing up she said, "You're so brave and I'm glad your back!" Her smile melted into her rosy cheeks. She stepped back to give Elizabeth some breathing room. "I'm sorry, I'm just so glad to see you!"

Elizabeth grabbed hold of the woman's hand and said, "Thank you, Mildred." Quickly letting go she added, "But it's only for today and then I'll be gone for a little while. I mean, I'll pop in here and there to take care of court for a couple victims but…"

Marilyn came towards her with a pleased look on her face. "I think I speak for the entire office when I say, we are very happy to see you and we're all so very proud of you." Her eyes twinkled with satisfaction.

Blushing, Elizabeth's eyes began to well with tears. Taking a breath, she fanned her face with her hand and said, "Okay, that's really about all I can handle."

Backing off and turning stern, Marylin said, "Everyone

get your coffee and bagels and let's get be back to work. It's Friday, but it's not five o'clock yet!" Nodding at Elizabeth, she turned and marched towards her office, out of sight.

As everyone went about their morning, Peggy walked past Elizabeth. Lacking emotion, she simply said, "Welcome back," before retreating to her own office.

Catching wind of it, China stared Peggy down as she walked away from them and rolled her eyes at Elizabeth. "Cankles," she quietly reminded her friend.

Appreciating China's effort of making Peggy less relevant than she needs to be, Elizabeth slightly giggled, careful not to disturb the stiches in her wound. The expression on her face turned into a thankful pout. "I love you."

Shrugging her shoulders China instantly responded, "I know." She winked, flung her hair off her brow, and strutted down the hall.

Having enough of the welcome celebration, Elizabeth grabbed her favorite flavored bagel, loaded it with cream cheese, and poured herself a cup of coffee. Marilyn only approved her to return for half the day and she had much to do.

The time went by much faster than expected. Before she knew it, China was knocking on her door. Peaking her head in, she reminded Elizabeth, "Hey you, it's almost noon and Marylin will have my ass if I don't get you out of here when the clock strikes."

Shuffling the documents in front of her as if she was

looking for something particular, she said, "I just need to finish this one thing."

Opening the door further and taking a step forward, China looked at her in a scolding manner. "*Liz…*"

Smiling as she looked up from the files, she took a breath and exhaled. She pushed herself from the desk and gave in. "Okay – *okay*! I'm done."

"It will all be here when you get back. And it's not like I can't call you if I need something," China toyed.

"I know, I just – I just feel guilty piling all this on you." She shrugged.

Shaking her head, China walked around the corner of the desk and grabbed Elizabeth's hand to drag her from the chair. "Nope, nope, nope! We're not doing this. Come on."

Like a child being drug from the playground, Elizabeth stood up pointing her finger and promising, "I *will* be back for the Sara Brewer trial."

China reached for Elizabeth's coat and her bag and held them out in front of her. "Of *course* you will, honey." Cocking her head, she smiled.

Smirking, Elizabeth took her purse and slung it over her shoulder before wrapping her arms around China's neck and hugging her. "I love you!"

"I love you!" China exclaimed. Shoving Elizabeth's coat at her, she said. "Alright, time to go. Don't even think about this place for a while."

Walking away from the pile on her desk, she said, "I'm

just going to tell everyone good bye and then I'm meeting Angel for lunch."

Leaning against the wall in the hallway, China crossed her arms in front of her as her eyes followed her friend out. "Perfect. I'll just be here, picking up your slack."

Elizabeth turned around with a playful look of offense. "I will talk to you soon…"

Laughing, China waved her hand and headed towards her office. "You better!"

Making her way through to the front, Elizabeth made a point to say something to everyone before she left. Thankfully, Peggy had gone to the courthouse and her snideness was avoided.

Once on the elevator, she leaned against the glass wall and rested her head back, closing her eyes until it reached the first-floor lobby. Her shoes clicked on the floor and as she turned the corner, she saw Danielle rise from the bench near the exit. She looked different than any other time Elizabeth had encountered her. Somewhat surprised, she greeted her. "Danielle? Hello! How are you?"

Embarrassed at her casual look, Danielle smiled and said, "Yeah, it's my day off. I called earlier in the week. The secretary said you would be in today and I wanted to personally thank you and see how *you* were."

Reaching out, Elizabeth gently touched her arm. "Thank you, Danielle. That really means a lot to me. I'm good. Still healing. But I'm good considering. How are you and how is Richard?" She sat down on the bench and motioned for Danielle to join her.

Talking a deep breath and sitting down, she replied, "We're good. Still healing." She smiled.

"It's a process. Not always an enjoyable one, but a process non-the-less."

Nodding her head, Danielle agreed. "But we're good. Richard and I actually decided we're going to start planning the wedding, if that's any indication."

"Oh my gosh! How exciting!"

"Yeah, we figured we needed something positive to focus on to get us through. Of course, it won't happen until we're *absolutely* done with Michelle's case and now, of course, the federal case. But once we have a solid date, we would really like for you to come?"

"I would love that," she said, blushing slightly. "Speaking of, I hear the AG's office is sticking to their word and giving you and Richard immunity in exchange for your testimony against Steve?"

She shook her head modestly. "They are. If it weren't for you and Marilyn, that may not have been possible." Not trying to show her vulnerability, she quickly changed the subject. "So, when I called the secretary said you were taking time off to study for the bar exam?"

A tad embarrassed Elizabeth replied, "Ah, I am. I'm hoping to expand the victim assistance division to include a victim rights attorney," she said proudly.

Danielle's lips fanned across her pale cheeks. "I think you'll make a great attorney. I'm sure there are a lot of women out there who need someone like you on their side."

A humble smile formed across Elizabeth's lips.

Standing from her seat, Danielle said, "Well, hey, I don't wanna keep you any longer than I should."

Following Danielle's lead, Elizabeth stood up and said, "I will be in the office here and there. And you have my number if you need anything or have any questions about what is going on. We can't talk directly about the cases, but -"

"I'm sure I'll be fine." Danielle took Elizabeth's hand in hers and with sincerity in her voice, she said, "Elizabeth, thank you for everything."

Elizabeth smiled as Danielle dropped her hand, turned from her, and headed towards the exit. Danielle glanced behind her.

Raising her hand, Elizabeth softly said, "Bye…"

DRIVING to the other side of town towards her house, Elizabeth headed to Terry's Tavern to meet Martinez. She was in the best mood she had seen since leaving the hospital. She turned the stereo up, singing along to the music as her thumb drummed the steering wheel.

Approaching the tavern, she slowed down and pulled her vehicle into the gravel parking lot. The air was chilly as the breeze reached her from the lake across the street. With energy in her step, she quickly reached the door and entered. Just inside, Martinez stood from his seat at the bar, flashing his perfect whites as he greeted her.

Kissing her cheek, his voice rang with excitement, "Hola, bella!"

"Hola yourself, handsome!" Looking over at the beer bottle in front of his seat, she flirted, "Starting the weekend early, are we?"

He laughed. "Hey, I took the rest of the day off. So, yes."

"Not judging. I'm always down for a little day drinking." She winked.

Elizabeth ordered a drink from the bartender and followed Martinez to a table in the corner with a nice view of the lake. Before she could remove her coat and sit, the bartender placed her beer on the table. She thanked her as she sat down.

Grabbing the menus from between the wall and the condiments and handing one to Elizabeth, Martinez said, "I have our whole weekend planned."

She graciously accepted the single, laminated page and curiously said, "Is that right? And what might that be, or is it a surprise?"

"Not – at – all. After lunch, we do whatever it is that Elizabeth Strong's little heart desires." His eyes teased hers before focusing on the menu.

Scanning the list of entrées, she said, "I think I have some ideas." She glanced up, coyly, just in time to catch him nod his head approvingly.

"I talked to Chico last night. I guess Johnson is ready to flip on Robinson and the whole outlet. It appears he's not quite liking the idea of joining several hundred or so inmates that he helped put away over the course of his career."

Instantly becoming upset, her demeanor became stand-offish. "What the hell does that mean?"

"No se preocupe, hermosa! He's not getting off on anything. Neither is Steve Robinson. Trust me, between the state and federal charges, Johnson and Robinson will never see freedom as we know it, *ever* again." Taking a celebratory swig of his beer, he continued, "I'm sure Johnson is just trying to make sure he's not placed in gen-pop and has a nice, cozy little cell to call home for the next 40-some years." He gave her a look of indignation.

The bartender interrupted the conversation. "You guys ready to order or do you need some more time?"

Shaking off her insecurity, Elizabeth said, "Yeah, I'll have the fried shrimp basket and could I get tartar and cocktail sauce, please? Thanks."

Taking Elizabeth's menu, Martinez placed them back in their spot against the wall and politely said, "And I will have Terry's burger, medium, with fries please. Gracias."

As the girl walked away to place the order with the kitchen, Elizabeth sat back in her chair, her expression became somber as she looked out at the cloudy sky above the choppy water.

Tilting his head, he said, "Hey, everything is gonna work itself out. You know that, right?"

Taking a deep breath, she straightened her posture before nodding her head at him.

Martinez was carful with his approach in asking her,

"I'm not sure if I should ask but, have you called Dr. Baker?"

Somewhat sarcastic in her response, she said, "It's okay. You'll be happy to know, I have a standing appointment every Monday for the next few weeks."

"Sorry, I won't ask again."

The bartender walked over to the table and placed a red basket full of food in front of each of them.

"Oh, thank God. I am starving!" said Elizabeth, happily embracing the change of topic.

Placing his paper napkin on his lap Martinez chuckled and said, "Well that was a nice segue."

Dunking a piece of shrimp into the tartar sauce before popping it into her mouth, Elizabeth said, "In other news, Marta and Bill are super excited to have you for Thanksgiving Dinner."

Having just taken a bite of his burger, he quickly chewed and wiped the ketchup from his mouth. His mouth still half full, he muttered, "They really like me, don't they?"

Finally, a giggle purred from her throat. "Yes – yes they do." As she twirled another piece of shrimp in the sauce container, she bravely offered, "So, I have been thinking that maybe after my studying and taking the exam, we could possibly discuss you getting rid of that shitty little apartment of yours?"

The expression of his face turned to stoned amazement. As a smile slowly formed across his lips, he slapped his burger in the basket and jumped from his chair hollering, "¡Ay, caramba!"

Laughter bellowed from her gut and she grabbed her side as she pleaded, "Don't make me laugh!"

He looked over to the bartender and to the other few patrons in the tavern and said, "Sorry! My apologies!" He sat back down, placed his hand over his heart and begged, "Are you kidding me right now? Elizabeth Strong, please tell me you're not kidding?"

She took a swig of her beer, licked her lips, and smiled at him as she slowly shook her head in the negative.

A NOTE FROM THE AUTHOR

Dear readers,

Thank you so much for reading! Really – *truly* – thank you.

I hope you enjoyed this series as much I loved creating it. Every single one of these characters holds a special place in my heart and I am so glad I could share them with you.

I had a story in mind years ago and it morphed into this crazy series that took me three books to complete. It also took a lot of blood, sweat, and tears, in order for it to become what is currently presented to you.

For more information or latest news, please visit www.kcturnerauthor.com or www.emhandly.com

Follow me on socials, E.M. Handly @edahandly

www.ingramcontent.com/pod-product-compliance
Lightning Source LLC
Chambersburg PA
CBHW061615100726
47898CB00002B/673